Love You to Pieces

by

Jerri Drennen

The Talking Dead Series

Cover Art by *The Wild Rose Press, Inc.*

The Wild Rose Press, Inc.
PO Box 708
Adams Basin, NY 14410-0708
Visit us at www.thewildrosepress.com

Publishing History
First Edition, 2025
Trade Paperback Print ISBN 978-1-5092-6390-5
Digital ISBN 978-1-5092-6391-2

The Talking Dead Series
Published in the United States of America

Dedication

This book is dedicated to my daughter Hanna who loves horror and asked me to try my hand at writing something darker than I'm accustomed to.

Chapter One

Taylor McClain stepped onto the treadmill and set the speed, preoccupied with the upcoming weekend. Camila, her best friend, was getting married, an event they'd been planning for well over a year. Sixteen months of venue touring, guest list revising, and invitation sending, then lastly, confirming numbers. Once that had been established, next came the menu for the reception, tasting entrée after entrée, and consuming twenty different decadent cakes, the reason she had to spend an extra thirty minutes every day at the gym to fit into her slinky, rose-colored bridesmaid dress.

She, Camila, and her best friend's mother had toiled endlessly to get every detail down and checked off, all leading up to an event that would shine like a diamond in everyone's memory as being the best wedding ever attended. At least that was the goal and something Taylor never wanted to do again. Being maid of honor was too time-consuming, especially with her full-time job. Every waking moment had been filled to the point she could barely breathe, let alone have any social life, and was the reason she was going stag. Taylor was the only one of Camila's wedding party without a date. *Yay. Good times.*

She drew in a frustrated breath and ramped up the speed on the machine. One thing she could do was look *hot* walking down that aisle since several single men were invited. Maybe she'd connect with one.

Minute by minute, mile after mile ticked by. Perspiration coated her forehead and beaded down her back as she pushed her body to the limit. After all, no pain, no gain, and she couldn't gain even an ounce the next four days.

At the forty-minute mark, she slowed the pace to cool down, giving her a chance to glance around the room. This early, not many were working out, but there were a handful of men and women, all sizes, shapes, and ages. One guy, standing over a man lifting weights, caught her attention—a tall, dishwater blond, built like a brick wall, in a pair of bicycle shorts and a sleeveless, muscle shirt that read Birmingham Gym. One of the personal trainers. The only reason she noticed him was his dark, intense eyes were on her, not on the man he was supposed to be spotting. Not very professional and sort of creepy, but then again, she thought any man who worked their body to that point was overcompensating for something. Probably a micro-penis. Steroids tended to do that to a man, not to mention giving them a serious case of roid rage. Who in their right mind would want to deal with that? Certainly not her. Being fit was okay, having a rhino neck wasn't.

Taylor returned her focus to the treadmill, noting the time, then pressed stop. She'd collect her stuff from the locker room and run home to shower. She still had a full day ahead and would need to make a pit stop at her favorite coffeehouse on her way to work, for some much-needed caffeine. The Perks was a great hangout for her and her friends; their frappes and cappuccinos the best anywhere in town. Today, she'd have to settle for the house blend, no sugar or cream. Black, strong, and zero calories.

As she stepped out the door, the chilly air caused goose bumps to form on her arms, though after her workout it helped cool her down. She glanced up and noted that one of the lights on the streetlamp had been broken out, making it darker than usual. Was it like that when she entered? She couldn't remember.

Her heart rate pitched as she clicked the fob on her key ring, her sedan in an area with little to no light. She rushed for the driver's door. Taylor should have been more persistent about talking her girlfriends into going this morning.

When she reached for the handle on the door, someone grabbed her by the shoulder and clamped on tight.

Taylor froze as his other hand slammed over her mouth. She bucked but couldn't get any leverage. Her body instinctively went taut, causing a charley horse in her calf.

With physical force she couldn't counter, she was dragged backward, her heels digging into the pavement, one of her tennis shoes slipping off. Bile rose in her throat and left a bad taste in her mouth, making it impossible to scream through his hand.

She scratched and clawed at his forearms. Yet his grip tightened, squeezing her so hard she could barely gasp for air.

To her left, a green, industrial dumpster came into view and ramped up her terror. This creep was trying to get her behind it so no one would see them. No way! She had to break free or she'd probably die, or at the very least be assaulted.

She kicked and flailed, super-human strength she didn't know she possessed energizing her. One of her jabs hit the mark, and he grunted in pain. His grip loosened for a second, and she jerked away and bolted forward, shouting for help. She frantically raced toward the building, only to be struck by his closed fist across her right cheek, stars dancing in the back of her eyes. Another blow hit her square in the mouth, a metallic taste making her gag. He then grabbed her by the hair and dragged her back, the pain more than she could bear. An agonizing wail broke loose. What was he going to do to her? She couldn't imagine. Or worse, she could.

His big hands wrapped around her throat and cut off her breathing. Pure, unadulterated panic set in, her thoughts on all that work she and her best friend had endured and she'd never get to see the results. Never witnessing Camila happily married was the last thought she had before everything went black.

****

Detective Reed Brentwood parked his car in front of a row of flashing police vehicles and rubbed at his overtired eyes. He was working on fewer than two hours of sleep. Hell, he'd barely gotten home when he'd been summoned to the scene.

Off in the distance, the faint hint of light crested, though it'd still be a good hour before the sun would come up. In his hand was a cup of coffee he'd gotten at a nearby convenience store. Hardly the best brew he'd had, but better than the precinct's.

He ducked under the yellow tape strung out behind a gym complex, a place you'd normally never catch him. Reed didn't have time to sleep, let alone work out.

He made his way to a pair of uniformed officers standing beneath the only streetlight. "So, what do we have?"

"Attempted murder. Would have been a sure thing had the paramedics not managed to revive her. Apparently, she's not out of the woods yet," the officer closest to him said. "They transferred her to Holy Trinity."

Reed released a relieved breath. "Do we know who she is?"

"Yeah, we found her purse lying on the ground next to her car. Name's Taylor McClain. She's a local. Lives off Mandolin. She has a membership here at the gym."

"Anyone see anything?"

"An older man by the name of Randall Morris said he came out of the gym and saw her feet sticking out next to the dumpster. As he got closer, a shadowy figure took off in the direction of Shrewsdale. He couldn't get a good look at him. Only that he was a big guy."

"Tall or wide?" Reed asked.

"Both."

Reed scratched at his stubbled chin. "Okay. We have any evidence at the scene?"

"Not any we could see. We have a crew gridding it right now. We'll let you know if they find anything."

"All right, then." He tapped his fingers against his gray sports jacket. "I guess I'll head over to the hospital and see what I can find out there."

Reed retraced his steps back to the car, trying to recall if they had any cases like this one. Sylvia Moore's could be since Taylor's attacker had been interrupted. Sylvia hadn't been as lucky. Her murder was still unsolved, gruesome because of her missing breasts, sliced clean off her body. Luckily, after she'd been strangled to death, according to the coroner. The mere memory of that crime scene still haunted him.

Inside his car, he shook his head, pictures of the lovely woman flashing through his mind. He'd never get over *her* murder as long as he lived. Whoever killed her was one sick puppy, and if it took him a lifetime, Reed planned to find him and make sure he paid the ultimate price for such a heinous crime.

The drive to the hospital was quick and uneventful, traffic light because of the early hour. He turned into the underground parking area and was forced to go up to the second level to find a parking spot.

Before leaving his car, he turned on the interior light above his head and worked up some notes on what they knew so far. He wanted to go in prepared in case he was able to speak with the victim—a long shot for sure, but he didn't want to be left unprepared if she was conscious.

He exited his black cruiser and headed for the steps. On the ground floor, he entered the hospital and walked up to the nurse's station. A pretty blonde in blue scrubs that had, of all things, llamas on her top, sat at the long nurse's station, talking to someone on the phone. When she looked up, her amber eyes widened before she ended her call.

He smiled. "A young woman was brought in about an hour ago. She'd been attacked. Can you tell me how she's doing?"

"Are you a relative?" the nurse asked.

Reed quickly flashed his badge. "I'm Detective Brentwood."

"Oh, okay. Let me see if I can get someone to talk to you. Give me a sec." She picked up the phone again, pressed in an extension, then relayed his need to speak to someone in charge of the woman's case.

"They'll be with you shortly. You're welcome to

take a seat in the waiting area if you'd like."

Reed nodded and stepped inside the glass-enclosed room filled with bright-orange chairs. On the TV in the corner, the early morning news anchor was talking about some fire on Belmont. He took a seat next to the table that held an assortment of magazines. He had a choice between *Better Homes & Gardens* or *Field and Stream*. Neither piqued his interest. Instead, he took out his phone to see if he had any messages. Just as he was opening one, a doctor stepped into the room.

"Detective? I'm Dr. Jaipal, Ms. McClain's doctor." The man was young, in navy-blue scrubs, and wore thick, dark-rimmed glasses.

Reed got up to shake the doctor's hand. "I came to see if Ms. McClain was conscious. We have a short window to catch her attacker, and I'd like to talk to her if possible. See what she remembers."

"I understand that, Detective, but she's in no shape for anything of that nature, right now. She coded again once she got to the hospital. We finally got her stable, but there's no way she'll be able to speak to you anyway since her windpipe was severely damaged. She's still struggling to breathe."

"So, she was strangled?" He took out his notebook and jotted down the information.

"That, and she had a three-inch cut along her scalp line we had to suture. We were able to get some DNA from under her nails and had it sent over to the crime lab. Why don't you give me your card, and I'll call when she's well enough to see you?"

Reed reached inside his breast pocket, retrieved one, and handed it to him. "The sooner the better. I have a guy out there who needs to be found before he can do this to someone else. Can I get one of your cards as well, just in case I have more questions?"

The doctor pulled a card out of his white coat and handed it to him. "I'll call you as soon as she's conscious and able to respond."

"Thanks for seeing me. Also, could you see that she doesn't have any visitors until I see her?"

The doctor nodded then left the room.

Reed was back to square one. Not at all a good start to an attempted murder investigation. But then, he'd caught suspects with less, and he hoped that'd be the case here.

Chapter Two

Taylor struggled to swallow, her throat so dry she almost choked, causing it to tighten until she could barely breathe. She glanced around the bed. The walls were white, which meant she wasn't home. Her condo had vibrant color everywhere.

There was a metal nightstand next to her, with three drawers, and on top, a large, plastic cup with a straw, along with something that looked like a remote connected to a cord.

"I see you're awake." A petite redhead with big blue eyes, wearing a pale-purple top and matching pants stepped next to the bed and smiled at her. Hanging over the woman's neck was a stethoscope and on her chest was a tag that read, Grace.

A nurse. I'm in a hospital.

Memories of the attack came rushing back, causing her heart to race so hard it hurt.

"Are you okay? Do you need a sip of water?" the nurse asked, those blue eyes now filled with concern.

Taylor nodded, then took a small sip from the straw put to her lips. She coughed and sputtered, trying to force the water down.

"It's going to be hard to swallow for a while. I'll go get you something for the pain. I'll be right back."

Tears filled her eyes. What had she done to deserve this? Nothing that she could think of. But at least she was alive.

The nurse returned and injected a hypodermic needle into the IV taped to Taylor's arm. "You should feel some relief soon. With time, it'll get easier. You'll just have to be patient."

Unfortunately, she didn't have time. She had a wedding to attend in a few days—at least she thought she did. How long had she been here? She tried to ask but nothing came out. *Oh God.* She had no voice.

A man in blue scrubs and a white coat came strolling through the door and stopped next to the bed. He had olive-colored skin, intriguing gray eyes, and straight, stunningly white teeth that were highlighted by his dark complexion. "Hello," he said in a low timbre, a tone that made her feel at ease. "Grace gave me the heads-up that you were awake. I'm Dr. Jaipal. I've been taking care of you since you came in yesterday morning. I don't want you to even try to speak right now so you can nod if you agree, shake your head if you don't. Do you understand?"

Taylor nodded.

He smiled. "Okay, good. Are you feeling any pain now?"

She shook her head. Since Grace had given her something, all she felt was numb inside.

"Glad to hear that. Do you remember what happened to you?"

She nodded, though she wished she couldn't. The whole thing had been so horrible that she wanted to block it out.

"Tomorrow, a detective is going to come by to talk to you about the events leading up to your arrival. I can hold him off another day if you'd prefer? It's up to you.

Are you okay with that?"

She wasn't, not really, but she wanted the man who'd hurt her caught. He deserved to be in jail. So, she nodded her head.

"Great. I'll call him when I get back to my office. You try to get some rest."

Hadn't she just woken up? Was she ready to go back to sleep yet?

"I'll be by in the morning before the detective comes. Take good care of her, Grace."

"I will. See you later, Doctor J."

The man left.

Taylor took a hard breath, lay back against the uncomfortable pillow and squeezed her eyes shut, reliving large hands gripping her throat, cutting off her air until everything went black. What occurred after that? Nope. *Don't think about that.*

How long would she have these terrifying flashbacks? A week? A month? A year? God, she hoped not.

Before yesterday, nothing fazed her; now she was scared to close her eyes.

She turned her head to find the nurse had gone and she was alone with her troubling thoughts.

Through the door, she caught sight of a pale, older man in a hospital gown walking by. His eyes connected with hers. He stopped, stared for the longest time, then abruptly took off again, leaving Taylor to wonder why he'd looked at her so strangely.

She shrugged and reached for the remote on the nightstand. Maybe some TV would calm her frazzled nerves?

Then another thought hit her, what if the sight of her

was why the man had stared? Could she look that ghastly?

Taylor reached up to feel her face, flinching when she touched her cheek. It felt swollen. So did her lip. And an odd, numbing sensation made her try to rub at her forehead, instant pain making her draw back. What had happened? She traced the gauze bandage along her scalp, her finger brushing against tiny, sharp edges underneath. Was it stitches? How had she cut herself, and how horrible did it look?

She needed a mirror.

A door to her left must be the bathroom. Bathrooms had mirrors. Did she have the strength to get up and walk over to see?

Taylor sighed.

All of a sudden, she didn't want to. She wasn't ready for the sight that might meet her. No way could she be maid of honor at her best friend's wedding. Camila didn't deserve that. Wedding pictures alone would be uncomfortable. Taylor couldn't imagine it. She'd need to bow out now so someone else could step in. But how could she let Camila know? Where was her phone?

She studied the remote for a call button.

Tears clouded her eyes again and blurred her vision. Then, her throat clogged as she draped her arm over her face, flinching again from the pain. She jerked it away, anger taking hold. Whoever did this to her needed to suffer. Over a year of her life she'd spent planning a wedding she wasn't going to get to attend because of some sick creep. The more she dwelled, the more furious she became, which wasn't doing her any good. She needed to calm down and allow her body to heal, then she could concentrate on getting even—now she just had to get better and hope the police caught the guy who did this to her.

****

Reed was losing patience with this investigation. Nothing seemed to be going his way. He'd arrived back on the scene this morning to learn that four different sets of shoe prints were found behind the dumpster. Not surprising considering the trash container was used by all the businesses in the strip mall. Yet, they'd still take photos in case they got a suspect. Then they could compare the prints against any of the man's shoes.

Earlier, at the precinct, he'd learned that there was no match from the DNA under the victim's nails. So, whoever attacked her wasn't in the system.

Reed's next step was to speak to the other people who'd been in the gym at the same time as his victim and weed out any that hadn't left before her. Those who were still in the facility when she was discovered would of course be eliminated. Though, they might still have info as to if anyone had been watching Ms. McClain, talked to her, had any confrontation with her while she was there.

He glanced at the list. Reed was going to talk to the man who found her last. That left seven others, including one of the gym's staff.

On that list, strangely enough, was a woman by the name of Katherine Fellows who lived on the second floor of his apartment complex.

Why would she come all the way over here to this gym when he was sure there were closer places? Odd for sure. But she'd now be last since he could talk to her on his way home.

Leanne Smith lived a block over, so he'd walk the

distance. As he did, he took in the fresh, cool air, opening up his lungs, reviving his senses. This helped him wake up since he hadn't slept but a couple of hours in days. Not that he hadn't tried. Insomnia had become his constant companion the past four months. Since there wasn't a match for DNA and Sylvia's case yielded no evidence at all. Not a fiber, finger or footprint. Yet, somehow he'd need to get a few hours of sleep before meeting with the victim of this crime.

At Leanne's front door, a little girl stuck her head out the side window, her big, liquid blue eyes reminding him of the Caribbean Sea. A highlight of the one and only vacation he'd ever taken. Alone.

He rang the bell and continued to watch the child, who looked leery yet gave him a toothy grin, a smile that revealed a missing front tooth. That suggested she had to be six or seven, and he only knew that because his niece was that age and had just lost her first tooth.

A blonde woman appearing to be in her mid-twenties answered the door, her eyes almost the same color as the child's, no doubt her mother.

Reed flashed his badge. "Are you Leanne Smith?

The woman nodded.

"I'm Detective Brentwood. I'm following up on the events at the gym yesterday morning. May I ask you a few questions?"

"Of course. I really don't know what I can tell you that would be helpful. I didn't see anything. I don't know the victim and didn't even notice that she was there."

"Are you sure?" Reed took out the photo that they had copied from Ms. McClain's license and showed it to her.

"Nope. Sorry, I've never seen her at the gym before.

I don't usually go that early, but my daughter was off from school, and I had my husband watch her so I could work out before he had to go to work."

Reed tried to gauge if she was telling the truth. He didn't see any deception. "Okay. Thank you for your time." He smiled at the little girl on his way to the door, then as an afterthought, turned back to the woman and handed her one of his cards. "If anything, no matter how small comes to you, give me a call."

"I will." She led him out the door, then closed it behind him.

One down, six to go.

Reed walked back to retrieve his car, glancing at the next person on the list. Herman Litman. Off of Cramer. Before heading in that direction, he needed to stop and get another cup of coffee. The crap he'd had at the precinct went untouched after the first bitter sip. Why couldn't they spring for better coffee?

At *The Perk* he found a parking spot and got out, opening the door for a teenage girl who was also going inside.

She smiled and thanked him.

In line, he glanced around, noticing the eclectic group of people. Reed had heard of the coffee joint before but had never come in. Usually, he was on the other side of the city where surprisingly most of the crimes were committed. Everyone here looked younger than him, the tables filled with men and women on their laptops and smartphones, drinking those fancy concoctions that Reed had no desire to drink. His coffee was simple. Black with no sugar.

He quickly ordered and paid the barista. Outside again, he took a sip and was pleasantly surprised at how good it tasted. He may just have to come back now.

The drive to Mr. Litman's took ten minutes. The man lived in a small, single-story home, in need of a paint job and a grass cutting. Yet the guy had time to go to the gym. *Priorities.*

He stepped onto the creaky porch and knocked since there was no ringer. After a moment, he rapped on the door again. Still no answer. Clearly, Litman wasn't home or he was still sleeping. Reed would have to put an asterisk next to his name and check back later.

Inside the car, his cell phone went off. He reached into pocket to find it was a number he didn't recognize but answered it. "Hello."

"Detective Brentwood?"

"Yes. Who's this?"

"Dr. Jaipal over at Holy Trinity. My patient is awake and is willing to talk to you in the morning if that works for you?"

"Yes. That works fine." Finally, something was going right.

"I want to warn you that I don't want her trying to talk at this time. Her vocal cords need to repair themselves. Talking would slow that process down. So, you might want to curb your questions to yes or no, where she could nod or shake her head, or maybe have her write down the answers."

"Thank you for the heads-up, Doctor. I'll be there in the morning."

"All right. Have a good day."

"You, too." Reed ended the call and stuffed the phone back in his pocket. He'd need to bring an extra pad and pen for her tomorrow.

So, who was next on his list? Vince Silva. The

personal trainer. He lived about five blocks from the coffee shop.

He started the engine and shoved the car into gear, taking another long sip of his coffee. It was strong, just what he needed right now.

Sylvia Moore's case popped back into his head. Were these two attacks related? Dr. Jaipal had said Taylor had been strangled and had a large cut on her hairline. Could he have possible been trying to take another prize, like with Sylvia's breasts. Could it be the same guy? Or was he just grasping here? He couldn't be sure. But then, stranger things had connected cases.

He took the next right onto Canal Street and found that the personal trainer lived in an upscale apartment complex, with all the amenities, much nicer than Reed's place. Must be a lot of money in helping people achieve the perfect physique.

Reed didn't give two shits about that. He'd rather get an hour of sleep. Funny how you obsessed over things you weren't getting. Next, he'd be thinking about sex, something else he hadn't had in a long time.

He took the stairs up to the second floor. The trainer's apartment was the last apartment on the left.

At the door, he knocked, waiting only a moment before a big guy who looked like The Hulk, except he wasn't green, opened it. He leaned his massive shoulder against the frame; the long-sleeved shirt he wore looked two sizes too small. He stared at Reed like he was some pesky bug he wanted to squash.

"Yeah," he prompted sharply.

Reed could punch his lights out. *Arrogant prick.* He flashed his badge. "I'm Detective Brentwood. You were at the gym yesterday morning when that woman was attacked?"

"Yeah, so what? I don't know the chick. I didn't even notice her there." The jerk tried to end the conversation by closing the door, but Reed reached out to stop him. "While you were there, Mr. Silva, did you notice anyone leaving before the police arrived?"

"Nope. I was with a client. Sorry. Now, I need to get a few hours of sleep before I have to go back to work." He slammed the door in Reed's face.

Fucking asshole. This was the one thing Reed hated about his job, people who thought their time was more valuable than anyone else's. He'd learned that on his first day, back as a rookie, some ten years ago. People like Silva made his job harder, yet he'd managed to cut through the bullshit and worked his way up the ranks. The last two years had been with Homicide Division and attempted murder, a unit that was tough on a good day.

Lately, Reed barely functioned. Too many victims haunted him, too many families who were left to wonder how their loved one had suffered before they died. People who needed closure, and he had to be the one to give it to them. Sometimes that was too much for him to take. Today he was handling it.

Tomorrow, he might not.

Chapter Three

Taylor swallowed hard as she texted Camila from a nurse's phone and told her she had to bow out of the wedding. Her best friend's emotional text back just about crumbled her reserve.

—*Are you sure about this? We could postpone the wedding.*—

No way. Deposits would be lost, which meant thousands and thousands of dollars. Taylor wouldn't allow it.

—*I'm sure. I love you*— Taylor texted back, then handed it back to the nurse standing next to her bed. Once she left the room, Taylor muffled a sob with her hand then flinched from the pain. She hated the man who had done this to her. He'd ruined everything. But again, at least she was alive. She needed to be thankful for that.

Her attention went to the door where the older man from yesterday stood, his face today even more gaunt, his green eyes sunken and less clear. What was wrong with him? How was he able to get around the way he looked?

"Do you know where I am?" His eyes pleaded with her for answers.

Taylor shrugged, unable to say a word. Even if she could speak, she wouldn't know how to respond to the question. Did he have dementia? That could explain a lot.

He stepped inside the door. "I've been walking around all over the place. I don't know where to go."

Again, Taylor shrugged her shoulders. How could she tell him she couldn't talk?

While she was trying to figure out how to help him, he abruptly turned and left. Then, the nurse who lent her the phone returned and came to her bedside. "I need to check your vitals. The doctor wants to see if you are willing to take a walk down the hall and back. Do you think you'd be up for that?"

Taylor nodded.

Susan wrapped a blood pressure cuff around her arm and pumped it, then gently pressed a thermal thermometer to her forehead, removed the cuff, and typed everything into the laptop she'd brought in with her.

Taylor wanted so badly to ask the nurse about the man at her door, but she couldn't. Not being able to use her voice was driving her crazy.

"I'm going to get you another gown to put over the top of the one you have on so you won't have to worry about flashing anyone." Susan walked to the cabinet against the wall and lifted the handle, grabbing a gown from inside. "Also, when we finish the walk, Dr. Jaipal said you are welcome to take a shower as long as you wear a cap to keep your stitches and dressing from getting wet."

Taylor nodded vigorously. Feeling clean would lift her spirits, especially when she'd be having company this morning. The doctor first, then the detective working her case.

The nurse helped her out of bed, slipped her feet into a pair of booties, then unsnapped one side of the gown to stick the IV tubing through. Until she was able to drink and eat without pain, she'd have the bag and pole.

With the extra gown now covering her, the nurse wheeled them both through the door and started down the hall. "If at any time you feel lightheaded, let me know, and we'll head back."

She nodded, glad that no one seemed to be around. She still had no idea how bad she looked. No way was she ready to see other people's reactions to her.

As they came to the end of the hallway, an older woman walked by them as if they weren't even there. *Strange.* At least she hadn't stared at her like she was a monster. That would have been devastating.

They reversed course and started back toward her room, her breathing becoming labored, causing a light-heading feeling.

"Are you okay?" the nurse asked.

She nodded again. By the time they were back in the room, her head cleared, and she was struggling less to breathe. The walk had helped clear her lungs. If she could, later, after her visitors left, she'd take another turn around the ward. The sooner she regained her strength, the sooner she could go home.

The nurse helped her into the shower, her hair tucked under a shower cap, her IV pole stationed outside the stall. Taylor blocked the spray with her hand to keep water away from her face. All she'd need was to get an infection on top of everything else.

Once she toweled off and removed her cap, she donned the clean gown she'd been given, and snapped the sleeves, then wearily shuffled back to her bed. The whole time in the bathroom, she'd avoided the mirror, happy to see steam had fogged it up as she dressed. She wasn't ready to look at herself. There was plenty of time for that, once she was stronger. At home, when no one would be there to see her break down.

She was dozing off when the doctor came in and gave her a bright smile. God, she wished her teeth were that white.

"So, Susan told me you took a walk and a shower. That's great progress. Are you feeling better?"

Taylor nodded.

"Good. You keep this up, and I'll be kicking you out of here in another couple of days."

His words were music to her ears. If she had her way, she'd leave today. But if she couldn't swallow food yet, that wouldn't be a good idea.

"What we are going to do now is see how well you tolerate liquids, maybe a little broth. If that works, we'll step you up to Jell-O tomorrow. We'll be able to send you home once you can eat soft food without a problem."

Her heart sped up at the prospect, though the thought of trying to swallow even liquids caused her throat to tighten.

"Are you still up to seeing the detective today?" he asked, his warm eyes questioning.

She nodded again. Answering the detective's questions was key to catching the man who'd done this to her.

"Okay. Good. He's here, waiting to see you. So, I'll go ahead and send him in, and I'll see you later this afternoon."

He left, and Taylor inhaled deeply, the hairs on the back of her neck standing on-end. She knew she had to stay strong.

She took even, calming breaths, trying to prepare

herself for an onslaught of emotion.

A man emerged at the door, tall, possibly in his mid-thirties, with dark, short-cropped hair. His eyes were navy blue, a series of deep, laugh lines framing them. The dark circles beneath made him look like he'd been putting in a lot of extra hours, or he hadn't been sleeping.

Would she say he was handsome? She wasn't sure.

In his arms were stacks of paper.

When he smiled, the gesture didn't reach his eyes. He appeared guarded for sure, and that made it hard for her to feel comfortable with him.

"Hello." He stepped closer. "I'm Detective Brentwood. I've been assigned your case. I brought you some magazines and a tablet and pens. If you want to write down your answers to questions, this might go smoother."

At that moment, Taylor wanted to kiss the man right on those full lips of his. Why hadn't she thought of this sooner? It would have made things easier. She could have asked the nurse about the older man.

He laid the stuff on the side of the bed and took out a small pad and a pen from the inside pocket of his sports jacket. "Are you ready to get started?"

Taylor nodded, then tore open the pens and flipped the pad to the first sheet of paper.

"Do you remember what happened to you?"

She again nodded.

"Good. Do you know what time you left the gym?"

Taylor contemplated the question, playing back when she'd gone to the locker room to get her stuff. She had glanced at her phone.

Yes. It was a quarter after six. I checked because I still had to go home to shower and get ready for work,

Taylor wrote.

He moved next to the bed to see her answer. "What time did you get there then?"

I got there at five.

He glanced down at her answer and frowned. "Do you normally go this early and work out for that long?"

Taylor wrote *I don't always go that early, but I had a wedding coming up, and I'd been tasting a lot of cake. I was trying to work it off.*

He glanced again at the answer she wrote. "So, you're getting married? Can I get your fiancé's name?"

Taylor shook her head, then wrote, *"My best friend is, this weekend.*

"Okay. Tell me what happened when you left the gym."

She inhaled a breath, then wrote down everything she could remember before blacking out.

He read over her reply, then nodded and wrote notes on his pad.

She was glad because she didn't want him to notice how uneasy remembering the event made her.

"At any time did you see him?" he asked.

She quickly wrote. *No. All I can recall is that the attacker's arm wrapped around my waist was strong, his hands callused. That's all I remember. He didn't say a word. I was able to get a grunt when I scratched him. That was it.*

He read her response, then asked, "Anything else? How about any smell? Did he give off one?"

She thought about the question. The guy's hand did smell like he smoked. Taylor quickly scribbled that down and showed him.

"Good. That's important. We can use that."

He seemed pleased with her, and that made her happy with herself. They needed to catch this guy, and they needed to do it quickly. Being a smoker could narrow the search.

****

Reed studied Taylor, thinking even with a badly bruised cheek, swollen lip, and cut along her hairline, she was a beautiful woman. Her hair was a light brunette, shoulder-length with soft curls, eerily similar to Sylvia's. Their bone structures were also alike. If it was the same attacker, maybe he had a type. He'd contact Travis Sanders, a profiler friend, to get his take on this. Then he could look into any cases that could fit that profile in neighboring cities. Hell, they could have a serial killer on their hands. But he was getting ahead of himself. *One case at a time, Reed. One case at a time.*

"Okay, Ms. McClain, thank you for meeting with me. I know reliving these events couldn't be easy. If you remember something else, let the doctor know so he can call me. I'll come back to see you."

She raised her hand and wrote on the paper, turning it toward him.

"Your phone? I can get your purse and bring it to you later. Would that work?"

She nodded, then gave him a smile that sent a ripple of something strange through his extremities, a reaction he'd never experienced before with a victim. Then again, most were dead. His reaction in this case was annoying since Reed was lead detective, and that's all he could ever be.

"Okay, then. I'll see you tonight." He turned and left, angry that he'd allowed a mere gesture of friendliness to upend his composure. Probably just lack of sleep. A couple of hours weren't enough, not when he was getting older, and his body couldn't recover as quickly. When he was a rookie, he could sustain abusing himself mentally and physically. Not any longer.

Once he was back in his car, he slammed his head against the seat-rest and closed his eyes. Why was he not sleeping anymore? Yes, Sylvia's murder haunted him, but what could he do? So much time had passed with no solid leads. Not one person had seen her the night she was killed. Nobody at work or her apartment complex could tell him a thing. Every step he'd taken led to zip, and her image bombarded him frequently—more often since they'd put the case on the backburner. It was like she was trying to tell him something, yet he couldn't figure out what. *Damn it all to hell!*

Could Taylor McClain's memories be vital to finding Sylvia's killer?

He opened his eyes. Again, one case at a time. He still had leads to follow here, and that's what he was going to do.

Fifteen minutes later, he pulled into the parking area of the police station. Reed caught sight of a fellow officer, Brad Kander, who worked in the technical support unit. He rushed to greet him in the elevator, both going up to the sixth floor.

"Hey, Reed. How's the McClain case coming along?"

"Good. I talked to her this morning. I now have some things to go on. You didn't by chance, follow up on that email on Sylvia's computer, did you? I really want to know who that IP address belongs to."

"I sent it to someone who is better equipped to locate the address. My buddy said he'd try to get back to me by tomorrow."

"Could you make sure to call me when he does? I want to know who it was who sent that bizarre email." Reed still couldn't believe they hadn't found the message sooner. It'd been sitting in her junk file, suggesting to him that Sylvia herself hadn't seen the troubling note. Maybe if she had, she would have sought help.

He placed a hand on Reed's shoulder. "I know solving Sylvia's case is important, Reed. I'll call you as soon as I learn something."

"Thanks." The doors opened, and they both stepped out and went their separate ways.

Reed walked straight to his desk, checking to see if he had any notes on callbacks. He quickly went through the stack, finding one that made his stomach clench. Sylvia's parents. He had nothing he could tell them, a fact that made his hands fist tightly at his side. He'd failed them, and there wasn't a damned thing he could do about it. He'd had unsolved cases before, but hers physically hurt. Her parents were heartbroken by their one and only daughter's death. He had to find her killer.

Calling them back would have to happen, but he couldn't deal with it right now.

With that, he went down the hall to evidence. Reed would have to sign Ms. McClain's purse out of the evidence locker. No prints other than hers were found on it and so the handbag could be given back to the owner. He could understand why she'd want her things—they'd make her feel somewhat normal again. Her family and friends could stay in touch through text since she wasn't supposed to speak and wasn't allowed any visitors.

Purse in hand, he left the precinct again, rubbing at his tired eyes. He had no time to be weary. He had to keep going since time was everything with attempted murder/murder cases.

In his car, he took out his pad and glanced at the three people from yesterday who hadn't been home to question, Herman Litman, Gretchen Harting, and the man who found Taylor, Randall Morris. Hopefully, he could catch them all today so he could move on from the interview portion of the investigation and hopefully have a direction to follow.

Chapter Four

Terror filled her crystal-blue eyes, and she tried to scream. Nothing came out. Large, hairy fingers tightened their grip around her throat, leaving her lungs burning from lack of air. As she lay on the cold, damp ground, breathless, a shiny, serrated blade came down and sliced through her skin, the pain so intense, she wished she were dead.

Suddenly, she hovered over the scene, watching someone in a dark hoodie butchering her, blood dripping down her ribcage, pooling on the concrete beneath her. Off to the man's side was an open container, inside translucent chunks of ice.

What was it for?

A noise startled the man. He rushed to finish his gruesome task, placed something covered in blood on top of the ice, and snapped the top shut. Then, he stood, glanced around, and sprinted away. He left her lying there alone. Cold. Her eyes and mouth wide open. Blood now outlined her torso, cracks in the concrete filling with crimson, branching off like capillaries. Draining away any chance of life.

Taylor jerked awake, forcing out the air caught in her throat. She clutched at her chest, thrashing, fighting to sit up.

Jesus. What kind of dream was that? It was like sitting in a movie theatre, watching a madman snuff the life out of a woman. Someone she didn't know, though she did have similarities to Taylor. Her hair color was close, and the shape of her face, yet it hadn't been her.

So why did she have the nightmare?

Her skin warmed; her heart pounded so hard it hurt. Sweat coated her body, drenching her gown. Taylor grabbed for the call button remote and pressed it.

When the nurse arrived, her eyes widened, and she rushed out again.

Wait! Taylor screamed in her head.

The woman returned with a syringe and injected the clear liquid into her IV.

"Take even breaths, Taylor. Slow and easy." Her voice was calm and steadying.

Taylor inhaled, then let the breath out, repeating the process over and over until she could breathe normally again.

"Good. Can you tell me what happened?" the nurse asked, watching her intently.

A nightmare, she wrote down on her pad and showed it to the nurse, then gulped in more air.

"I guess you aren't up to having the detective come in, then?"

She grabbed the woman's arm before she sent him away. Taylor wanted her phone—needed her phone more than anything right now.

She quickly wrote that she wanted to see him.

"Are you sure?"

Taylor nodded.

"All right. As long as you're sure." She stood there, clearly wanting her to change her mind. Taylor wasn't going to. She needed to see the detective. Maybe the dream she'd had meant something. Perhaps he could make some sense of it all.

She brushed away the hair plastered to her face, assumed she looked dreadful, but right now, she didn't care.

The detective stepped into the room, an arm wrapped around Taylor's purse. "The nurse told me to make this brief."

Taylor didn't want that. Just him being here made her less scared. He came close to the bed and handed her the purse, then took a step back.

Intently, she watched him, noticing how tired he looked, how deflated.

She reached for the pad and pen, started writing down her dream, then she held it out to him.

He hesitated for a moment, then took the tablet and read what she'd written, his eyes widening, his jaw slacked.

"You just had this dream?" His voice sounded strained.

She nodded.

He handed the pad back and asked, "Can you tell me what the man or the woman looked like?"

Taylor wrote everything she could remember and gave the pad back. His eyes widened again and gave off a knowing gleam, but she wasn't sure why.

"You're telling me the woman looked like you but wasn't?"

She nodded again.

Taylor could tell his mind was working, which meant that perhaps her dream meant something to him. Hopefully, it could help catch the guy who'd done this to her.

But was this dream from the past, or was it some

premonition? Or nothing at all? Somehow, by the detective's reaction, it seemed relevant.

"Well, I guess I'd better go before I get kicked out of here." He handed the pad back to her. She reached for his hand instead, not wanting him to leave.

He looked at her, confused, somehow bothered by her touch.

She instantly let go, feeling stupid for thinking he'd want to stay. The man had a job to do, one that wasn't babysitting her and her emotional outbursts.

"Time to go." Her nurse walked into the room. "Visiting hours are over, and Taylor needs her rest."

That was the last thing *she* needed, yet Taylor didn't have a choice. Not if she was in the hospital. She'd need to remedy that. Hopefully, by tomorrow, she would be home, in her bed, then Taylor could do whatever she wanted. She wouldn't have to listen to any doctor or nurse tell her what to do any longer.

****

Reed left Taylor's room with the strangest feeling. The dream she'd had freaked him out, yes, then her hand, touching his, had sent every nerve in his body on high alert. The hair on the back of his neck still stood on end. Something about this woman made him edgy and unsettled.

His fricking electrical system was going haywire. He had to shake this, and he had to do it now. Solving this case was crucial, and Reed needed to be on top of his game. His reaction to her brief, yet somehow intimate caress, sent him into a tailspin, and he couldn't function. The only way to get over this was to stay away from her—get his brain back to overriding his body's response.

Reed took the stairs down to the ground floor. He pushed open the door into the parking garage, almost empty this time of night. As he walked toward his cruiser, a guy sitting in an SUV caught his attention, his instincts kicking in.

He started toward the vehicle just to talk to the man. As he got closer to the car, the guy in a black cap pulled down low and dark-tinted glasses started the vehicle and pulled away before Reed could reach him. What was up with that? Why leave so quickly? Was he nervous about talking to Reed? Something in his reaction didn't feel right.

He reached into his pocket to grab his pad and pen to try and get the license number when the guy turned a corner, only giving Reed a chance to get the last two digits. *Dammit, all to hell.* What was the guy doing? Or better yet, what had he intended to do?

What if he was here to get to Taylor? To finish the job. Now, she was going to need security.

He grabbed his phone and pressed the precinct. Until he could get it authorized, he'd stay and make sure nothing happened to her.

While Reed relayed his concerns to the chief, he headed back up to her floor, then down the hall. He made a pit stop at the nurse's station. The charge nurse stepped out of an office behind the angular desk and smiled at him. "Can I help you?"

He flashed his badge. "I'm going to need a chair to be placed outside Taylor McClain's room. I don't want her to know about it. It'll just scare her, and I'm sure nobody here wants that. Now that she's conscious and her attacker is on the loose, he might try to get to her here. Until we get a uniformed officer to stand guard, I'm going to stay."

The older woman nodded, then turned to walk back into the office, returning with an orange chair and handing it to him. "Coffee shop is open until ten if you want to get a cup before you settle in. Also, if you're still here by morning, the cafeteria opens at seven. They have great cinnamon rolls if you get there early enough."

He gave her a weak smile. "Thanks for the tip."

"You're welcome."

Reed toted the chair down the ward's hallway and placed it off to the side of Taylor's door. He'd need coffee, so he rushed to get a cup before the shop closed, then came back and sat down. It was going to be a long night, especially in this upright position. He sat sideways and leaned his shoulder against the wall, taking a sip of his coffee, watching the elevator doors. Those doors and the stairs were the only way to get to Taylor, and Reed had a clear view to both from his vantage point. They'd have to go through him to get to her.

Ten minutes led into an hour that led into two, and Reed still sat in the chair, his ass starting to go numb.

His phone chirped, and he pulled it from his breast pocket and saw that it was Brad Kander. He clicked on the text.

—The email address was from a guy who lived in Indiana. Name's Jeffrey Fillmore. He and Sylvia met on a dating app. I don't think there is any connection between this guy and her murder. I could see if my source could dig deeper if that's what you want. It's up to you.—

Reed rubbed at his tired eyes, contemplating what to do. Did it make any sense to go down that road? The guy lived hundreds of miles away.

—Don't bother. I think it'd be futile to do that.—

Reed texted back.

He tucked the phone in his pocket and leaned against the back of the chair, stretching his long legs out in front of him. He focused on the elevator doors again, a ding signaling an arrival. The doors slowly started to open.

Reed sat up and drew in a breath. He let it out when it was only a nurse arriving for her shift.

Damned if his nerves weren't a frazzled mess and being so close to Taylor McClain after their last encounter wasn't helping in the slightest.

Two hours of staring at those doors caused Reed's eyes to start to creep shut.

Someone kicking at his feet woke him. He opened his eyes to see an officer from his precinct standing there looking like he'd had ten hours of sleep.

"They sent me to relieve you," the younger cop said. His chipper attitude only annoyed Reed further and made him want to kick the guy back.

"Before I leave, I want you to know that if anything happens to Ms. McClain while she's in your detail, you'll answer to me. Understand?" While he was giving the stern rebuke, inside Reed was chiding himself for falling asleep. Now, before he left, he'd need to stick his head into Taylor's room, make sure she was all right. Something he wouldn't have had to do if he hadn't been so unprofessional and dozed off.

The smile on the man's face disappeared, along with a little of his color. "Yes, sir. You can trust me, sir."

"Good. I'll be back later today to make sure Ms. McClain is doing okay."

Reed didn't trust anyone but himself to watch her, however, he needed sleep, otherwise he wasn't going to be good for anything.

He rose, a sharp pain shooting up his spine. The next time he came, he would have to find a better chair because that one was torture. Then again, maybe the hospital would release Taylor today, and he wouldn't have to worry about it.

With that thought in mind, he stepped inside Taylor's room, relieved to see she was sleeping soundly. Then he left the hospital and headed home to get some much-needed rest and maybe to rub on a little pain relief cream for good measure.

Chapter Five

Taylor smiled, happy now that she could finally swallow soft food, and Dr. Jaipal was discharging her. She'd never been so relieved. The only bad thing about this was how she'd have all the reminders of Camila's wedding around her. From the long, clingy dress hanging from the back of the closet door, to the fancy, floral headband the bridesmaids were to wear. Earrings and necklace laid out on her vanity, everything she had needed for that special day—all shot to hell.

Tears filled her eyes, but she quickly brushed them away. Nothing was going to keep her from going home. It was her sanctuary, a place she'd worked hard to buy five years ago with the help of her grandfather's inheritance. She'd spent six months turning every room into a reflection of her personality. Finding the right paint colors and accent pieces to add to her home's eclectic charm. Everyone loved her place, and said she had the best taste. Many had even asked for her advice on decorating their own homes. Taylor had a flair, though it wasn't what she did for a living. No, that was the humdrum world of advertising, a job she'd had since graduating from college, and her love of interior design only helped in her field of work.

Taylor slipped into a pair of sweatpants and a T-shirt one of her friends had dropped off at the nurse's station. Taylor didn't know who. She hadn't been ready to see anyone and had asked Camila to relay that to all her friends. When she was ready, she'd deal with what happened and call. Until then, she needed her space, and she knew Camila would make sure her wishes were met. That's why they'd been best friends since middle school. They both respected one another and always listened when boundaries were crossed. Not easy since both she and Camila could be hard-headed, yet they'd managed to make it work for so many years. The reason why Taylor would never get over having to miss her wedding. Just the idea of not witnessing the union crushed her, but it had to be this way. She wasn't ready to deal with what happened, and she knew her friends would ask— impossible to ignore with her face having taken a beating. If their situations were reversed, she'd want to know. So, she couldn't blame them.

Weary, she stepped into a pair of white, slip-on tennis shoes, then sat on a chair in the corner waiting to be released. When she signed the papers, she'd call for an Uber.

Minutes ticked by, and her eyes started to droop, a knock causing her to sit up straight in the chair. She glanced at the door to find Detective Brentwood. If she thought he'd looked tired before, he looked even more so now.

"Heard you were getting released. Do you have someone coming to pick you up?"

She smiled, then rose to get her pad to write. *I am, and I'm planning to call for a rideshare.*

He stepped closer to read her response. "How about you let me drive you home? I'd feel better knowing you were there safe."

She frowned, then wrote, *I wouldn't want to put you*

out.

He smiled. *"It'd be my pleasure."*

Taylor wasn't sure why this man was going out of his way to help her, but she was appreciative. Being around him gave her strength. Why, she wasn't sure. Maybe his self-assurance, or his muscular build, how he'd be capable of physically protecting her if anything were to happen. Either way, she'd let him drive her home.

A nurse stepped around him. "Well, here you are. Free as a bird." She smiled at Taylor. "While you sign these papers, I'll go get a wheelchair to take you down. You do have a ride, don't you?"

"Yes," the detective said. "I'll go bring my car around to the front."

He left, and the nurse gave her a wink. "That man is quite the tall drink of water, isn't he? If only I were single." She flashed her ring finger where a small diamond sparkled.

Taylor hadn't looked at the detective that way. Safety was her only concern. Especially after being attacked.

Her nurse left the room while Taylor signed the release papers, returning a few minutes later with the wheelchair. Slowly, she rolled them to the elevator doors. As they waited, Dr. Jaipal came down the hall and spotted her. When he reached her side, he patted her shoulder. "It was a pleasure to take care of you, Taylor. If you have any problems, my extension is on your release papers. If you need anything, call me." He gave her a shoulder squeeze, his hand lingering overly long before he left them once the doors opened.

The nurse chuckled as they entered the elevator and

the doors closed again. "I don't believe I've ever heard Dr. J. say that to a patient. He's single, you know."

Taylor couldn't help but blush. Was the nurse trying to make her feel good, knowing that once she got home, she'd finally get a good look at herself? Probably, but it was sweet of her to say.

Outside the hospital doors, Detective Brentwood stood in front of a black, four-door sedan, holding the door open. She quickly got in and snapped the seatbelt in place.

Behind the wheel, he clicked his own across his broad chest.

She was going home, and that was all that mattered right now.

"Don't freak out, but I did get directions to your home while I brought the car around. I've never been on Mandolin, which must mean it's a safe place to live."

She wrote down her answer and turned the tablet toward him. *I believe so. I know all my neighbors. We all look out for each other.*

"That's good to hear." He pulled out of the hospital and started down the street.

Taylor wondered why he'd been happy to hear that about the people around her, but she shook it off. Nothing was going to dampen her spirits. She was going to be home soon.

"So, what do you do for a living, Ms. McClain?"

She wrote *Magazine and newspaper advertising* and showed him her answer.

"Do you like your job?"

She shrugged, then wrote, *It pays the bills. What about you? Surely, yours must be hard.*

He glanced at her answer and question, then said,

"Sometimes it is, yes."

Taylor could tell by his short answer this wasn't something he wanted to discuss.

For the remainder of the trip, she stared out the window, sweat forming on her back. Where was the man who'd done this to her? Why did she have that dream? Had the guy who attacked her been watching her, or had it been random? Did he know where she lived? What if he was waiting for her to get home.

Her breathing became labored, and she tried to think of something to ease her mind, but nothing came.

"Are you okay?" The detective glanced her way, his navy-blue eyes narrowing with concern.

She sucked in air, her chest tightening from the effort.

"Do you need me to take you back to the hospital?"

Taylor shook her head. That was the last thing she wanted.

She wrote down her concerns, hoping he'd be able to reassure her.

He quickly pulled onto Mandolin and parked in front of her home.

She handed him the tablet, and he read what she'd written, then looked at her.

"I'm going to be honest with you, Taylor, I have some concerns about who did this to you trying to get to you again, but I'm not going to let him. We had security outside the door of your room last night and this morning. An officer will be outside your house tonight. I plan to go inside with you now and check everything before I leave. I'll also give you my personal phone number. You can call me day or night. I don't think this guy will try anything during daylight hours. We'll keep you safe, Taylor, and we will catch him."

His words calmed her and for some reason, she trusted him, and that gave her confidence she would get through this nightmare.

****

With Taylor following close behind, Reed walked from room to room, checking every inch of her place. He knew from the look on her face she was terrified by the prospect of being left alone, but he'd reassure her that she'd be safe even if he had to stay with her himself.

"Everything looks clear." Reed gave her a weak smile. "And remember, I'm just a phone call away. In your case, a text message away." He scribbled something on a card and handed it to her. "If you have any questions, text me anytime. I will get back to you. Okay?"

All right, she wrote, still looking anxious. Reed felt bad leaving her, but he had a case to solve. He couldn't hang around here.

"It'll be all right. Keep all your windows and doors locked. He won't be able to get in, and by nightfall, there will be a patrol car out front until morning. I have to go. I'll let you know if I catch a break in the case."

She followed him to the door, her expression grim. He didn't know what else to do, to reassure her that she'd be safe.

"Lock the door when I leave."

She nodded and watched as he left, then closed the door.

Dammit. That haunted look on her face was going to torture him all day. But the only way to make her feel safe again was to get the guy who'd done this and put him behind bars.

Reed jumped into his sedan, started the engine, and pulled away from the curb. Right now, he needed to follow up on something Gretchen Harting had told him when she was working out. She'd noticed Ms. McClain on the treadmill before she'd been attacked and had also seen that Vince Silva had his eyes glued to her the whole time. And he'd lied about it. Reed was going to have another talk with Silva, find out why he'd told him he hadn't even noticed her. People lied for a reason. What was his motive? Was he afraid he'd become a suspect or was it something more sinister?

Ten minutes later, he was pulling up in front of the Birmingham Gym, a chain owned by William Birmingham, a fun fact he'd learned from one of the officers at the crime scene. Something Reed probably wouldn't need to know but now did.

He exited his car and stepped into the front door, flinching at the loud noises. The clanks and bangs alone would be reason enough not to come, though he noticed most of the occupants inside were wearing earbuds—no doubt listening to music or an audiobook.

He headed straight for the door that read *Office*, glancing at the people on his way, hoping to see Silva on the floor training someone. *Nope.*

Reed reached the office and stuck his head inside, spotting Silva lounging on the sofa, wearing a tight-fitting, long-sleeved shirt. Wouldn't he get hot in that? Most everyone else was wearing T-shirts and shorts. Could he be hiding something? Scratches, perhaps?

Too bad he couldn't come out and ask to see his arms without a warrant, and he doubted any judge would give him one without probable cause. This was a theory, nothing more.

"I need a word with you, Silva," he said when the man noticed him. "I have a few follow-up questions to ask."

The man's eyes darted around the room. Was he thinking of bolting? *Try it, asshole. See how far you get.*

Silva rose slowly and stepped out of the room. "Let's talk outside. It's too noisy in here."

Reed followed him out of the building and off to the right.

"So, what the hell do you want now? I told you, I don't know the chick," Silva snapped.

"You might not know her, but according to another member at this gym, you were staring at the victim on the morning of her attack. As I recall, you said you didn't even notice her. Did you lie to me, Mr. Silva?"

"Okay, I may have looked at her once or twice, but I didn't lay one hand on her. I was in a session. I was still in the building when the cops showed up. Are we done here?"

Reed clenched his teeth, causing his jaw to ache. This guy was as arrogant as they came. "Can you verify that?"

"I can check my records. See who I was training that morning."

"Let's do that." Reed pointed toward the door.

"I don't have my book here."

Reed didn't believe him for one minute, but what could he do? "Okay, so then where is it?"

"At home. I was running late this morning and forgot to grab it on my way out."

Reed studied the man intently. "Is this something that happens a lot? How do you know who you're training today without a record of it?"

"I hang around until a client shows up. At lunch, I'll run home and get it."

"So, you are saying, if I come back later today, your book and the name of the client will be available for me to follow up on?"

Silva's eyes darkened, and his mouth straightened into a severe line. "How about I just call you and give you the name."

"Okay." Reed reached inside his jacket to retrieve one of his cards. "You call me as soon as you know. There is a whack-job out there. We need to catch him before he tries to do this to someone else."

"Yeah, okay." Silva ripped the card out of Reed's hand, then stalked back inside the building.

Reed would have loved to follow him inside and prove who was the bigger man, but all that'd get him was a possible suspension. He didn't need that. One thing was for sure, Vince Silva fit the profile of a sociopath. Arrogant, self-involved, narcissistic. But he couldn't prove he was Ms. McClain's attacker—not yet at least. But if he was, he was going to get Silva and make him pay.

Chapter Six

From behind, someone grabbed her. A powerful grip burrowed into her arms. Fear kicked in, her need to get away becoming paramount. She sunk her nails deep into his flesh, a jerk from her attacker egging her on. She scratched and dug at his forearms while stomping on the inside of his foot. His grip loosened, allowing her an opportunity to escape. She sprinted down the alley. Heavy footfalls directly behind ramped up her adrenaline. She had to reach the street and flag someone down.

Her legs burned, her lungs ached, yet she refused to let up. Right as she neared the end of the alleyway, hands reached around her shoulders and pulled her back. She was spun around, then punched in the head, and she went down. The impact of the hard asphalt knocked the wind out of her. He then dragged her into the dark recesses of the alley, blinding her to everything. She couldn't see him. Couldn't fight. When they came to a stop, he dropped to his knees and wrapped his hands around her throat, tightening like a vice, squeezing the air from her lungs. She lay there, pawing at his arms, too weak to pry them away. Then she went limp, watched as he took a jagged-looking knife out of his boot, and started cutting into her skin. Strange that she couldn't feel anything now—didn't seem to care. Moments later, he left her, with blood pooling around her head, her body growing cold and rigid.

Taylor woke, her heart pounding in her chest like she'd run a 10k. Again, she was drenched in sweat, and her pajamas stuck to her skin. The woman in the dream had looked like her yet wasn't. Neither was she the woman from the first nightmare.

Why was she having these dreams? Could they be just bad dreams or something else? Like her troubled mind trying to work through what she'd endured at the hands of her assailant? Taylor wished she knew.

With her attack, she'd never seen the man, but in these dreams, he wore a black hoodie. And this time, she saw his boots. They were brown, with black shoelaces. Did that mean anything? Should she tell Detective Brentwood?

When she talked to him about her first dream, he'd seemed intrigued. Would he react the same to this one, and would her stomach again do that fluttery thing when she saw him leave her home that day?

Taylor took a calming breath and stood. After a shower, she'd get dressed. Sleep was totally out of the question now. Who could rest after that horror show?

In the bathroom, she searched in the vanity drawer for a shower cap. She knew she had one, but she rarely used it. Until the stitches came out, she'd need to, which meant she'd have to buy some dry shampoo, something Taylor had never used. Washing her hair had been a daily routine. So, she'd never required it before today.

Her gut clenched at the idea of going anywhere. She simply couldn't deal with the looks she'd get. The questioning stares and speculation. Most people couldn't. She'd have to order online.

Once she removed her damp pajamas, she stepped

into the stall, keeping a safe distance from the spray. Who were these women in her dreams? Were they related in some way to Taylor's attack? She wanted to know, but then again, did she? Her emotions were all over the place.

What if they were connected? From what she'd witnessed, these women didn't survive their attack. Had she been the lucky one?

Taylor forced the thought away. She was alive and planned to stay that way. Especially since she had Detective Reed to protect her. That man in the hoodie wouldn't be bold enough to try again. There were too many eyes on her now. Right?

She finished her shower and toweled off.

Her gaze was drawn to the clouded mirror.

Nope. She still wasn't ready. There was enough to deal with right now. Seeing how bad she looked could wait another day or two.

By the time she'd dressed, her emotions were on an even keel again, where they needed to be. Worrying about anything would only hinder her healing, and she wanted to get better as fast as she could. She may not be able to attend Camila's wedding, but she wanted to be one hundred percent for when her best friend returned from her honeymoon, to help her move into the couple's new home. An event she'd been tapped to do, to help decorate the two-bedroom house. A promise she made and one she'd keep no matter what—something she could look forward to doing. She needed that.

Taylor walked to the kitchen and quickly put on a pot of coffee, then retrieved her laptop. Her favorite online site would have the things she'd need, and they could be here in a couple of days.

Once she had finished, she poured herself a mug of coffee and left the kitchen, not knowing what to do with herself. She wandered around her condo, suddenly feeling lonely. Her friends were all busy with Camila's wedding prep and she really wasn't ready to speak to any of them yet anyway.

Frustrated, she walked over to a window and pushed the curtain aside to look out. A police cruiser was parked next to the curb, the officer inside leaning his head back against the headrest.

Taylor couldn't see if his eyes were open or not, but the mere thought of the cop being asleep charged the hairs on the back of her neck. If it were safe, she'd go out and see but the creep could be watching her right now, waiting for her to do something stupid.

She shoved the curtain back in place. If she was inside, she'd be safe. Wouldn't she?

Maybe she could text Detective Brentwood. Ask him to contact the police station to check on the officer.

A thump from the back of the house sent her heart racing. She tried to move but her limbs were locked in place. What was the noise, and what had caused it?

She held her breath, listening intently. Perhaps it was her imagination? She was letting it run wild.

Another bump made her jerk. She had to text for help.

She raced to find the card the detective had given her, her frantic thoughts making it much harder than it should've been. She couldn't remember where she'd placed his number. Why hadn't she instantly put it in her phone? Where was her phone? *Oh, God. Stay calm.*

In her mind, she replayed him handing her the card, how she'd held onto it until he'd gone, then took it and her purse to *her room.*

Was that where the sound came from?

She had to risk it.

Cautiously, she moved down the hall, then inched inside the room, her eyes straining to adjust to the darkness. Should she flip on the light? Would that deter anyone outside? The clock radio on her nightstand read quarter to five.

Seconds in, she could see an outline of her purse on the nightstand, and she raced to get it, a white card sitting next to it. She snatched both and scrambled toward the front of the house.

Back in the kitchen, she found her phone, pressed in his number, and waited. It rang, and rang, and rang, then went to voicemail. The man was probably sleeping, rest that he needed, the dark circles under his eyes making that clear. Besides, how was she going to talk to him with no voice?

Now what? Should she text him? No. It might wake him if indeed he was sleeping.

There hadn't been any more thumps. Perhaps it'd been nothing. Just sound amplified from stress.

She walked back to the front window, peered out, and noticed the officer was talking to someone on his radio. He was awake. *Thank God!*

****

Reed wanted to punch something as he stepped under the crime scene tape. Thirty minutes ago, he'd gotten the call. Another woman had been attacked, this one not as lucky as Taylor had been.

He met a young, uniformed officer halfway down the narrow alleyway, his grim expression all Reed needed to know. It was bad.

"Who was she?" Reed asked. "And who found her?"

"Jamie Danson. Twenty-seven. A dog was barking like crazy when Tad Fields was walking by. He came into the alley to investigate and found her body. The coroner is examining her now."

"Okay." He patted his back. "Thank you."

Reed knew rookies didn't do well with gruesome crime scenes. They needed some human contact to help them get through the hard sights. Reed had suffered early on, would've appreciated a higher-up helping him deal with some of the horrors he'd seen.

Reed strode over to where lights illuminated the area and found Ken Vogel, lead coroner, leaning over the woman's upper body.

"You got anything for me, Ken?" Reed glanced at his surroundings. The body was lying up against a series of pallets, impossible to see if not for the team's floodlights. How the woman's body was found even by a dog at this time of night was a miracle.

The crime scene unit were taking pictures of the victim and the area.

Ken looked up at him, giving Reed full view of the victim, and his stomach churned. She'd been scalped, bits of hair and skin still left around her ears and forehead.

Taylor's face popped into his mind. This could have been her had someone not interrupted them. Then, he remembered that Silva never got back to him about who the client was he'd been with. Could he be the killer? Was that why he'd been so evasive with Reed?

"You okay?" Ken's inquiry drew him back to the grisly scene.

"Yeah. Can you tell me anything?" He had to stay

focused because another murder of a vulnerable woman suggested a pattern. Possibly a serial killer, and he had to find him before he murdered again. Also, this new victim only placed Taylor's life more at risk. The killer wasn't going to leave any loose ends, and she was one of them. In his gut, Reed felt he'd need to step up surveillance on her.

"Her temp suggested she's been dead less than six hours. If I had to guess, four at the most. Marks around her neck indicate strangulation, but I won't know for sure until finishing her autopsy. Because of the blood pooling, all damage to her head was done before she was dead, or shortly thereafter."

"Was she sexually assaulted?"

Ken frowned. "I see no sign of that, but again, I'll be able to tell you more after the autopsy."

"Okay. Thanks, Ken. I'll check back with you later today."

Reed walked away from the scene, jotting down some notes, stopping to talk to another officer on the way to his car. "Has anyone contacted next of kin?"

"Yes. We sent an officer over to the family's home thirty minutes ago."

"All right. I'm going to check-in at the precinct. If anything else comes up, let me know."

"Yes, sir. I will."

While heading for his car, Reed tried hard to control his seething temper. No way could he let another woman die on his watch. If he'd only done more with Taylor's case, maybe Jamie would be alive now.

Reed opened his car door and slid in, thinking he'd stop by Taylor's before heading to the precinct. He wanted to make sure she was safe, check on the officer watching her, maybe bring him a cup of coffee.

Years ago, he'd done these types of details, doing surveillance on suspects, and protecting victims. He appreciated any officers bringing much-needed food and drink, especially for those overnight stints.

Before heading to her home, he pulled up to a twenty-four-hour coffee and donut shop. He quickly grabbed three cups of their French roast and a dozen assorted donuts in two boxes, then drove to Taylor's condo.

When he arrived, Reed pulled up behind the police cruiser, grabbed a cup of coffee, a box of donuts, and went to tap on his side window. The officer recognized him and pressed the roll-down button. "What brings you here this early?"

"I came by to bring you coffee and donuts and to check on our charge." Reed handed him the box and cup.

"You're a saint, Brentwood. Ms. McClain is probably still sleeping like most people are this time of the morning."

"I'm going to check on her since we had another woman murdered tonight. I'm afraid we are going to have to step up her protection around the clock. The killer might think she's a liability and try to finish the job."

The officer frowned. "Are we sure it's the same guy?"

"I'd bet my life on it. Keep your eyes open." Reed returned to his car for the other box of donuts and two coffees, then walked up to the door to knock.

Taylor opened to him immediately. Had she been watching from the window?

He gave her a weak smile. "Hey, can I come in?"

She moved aside to allow him inside, then closed the door.

"You been up awhile?" He handed her one of the coffees.

I had another bad dream that woke me, she wrote. *I couldn't go back to sleep. How about you? You look as if you've been up all night.*

She turned the pad for him to read.

"I don't get much rest in this job. Care to tell me about this dream that woke you?" Reed was curious since the last one she'd had was too close to Sylvia's murder to discount.

She took a sip of her coffee, smiled, then wrote.

This is good. Um, well, it was another woman getting strangled and cut up. She wasn't the same one from the first nightmare. She looked similar but different, you know?

"Can you see the person perpetrating this?"

She quickly wrote down her reply. *Again, he wore that black hoodie, so I couldn't see his face. On his feet were a pair of brown work boots, thick treads, with black shoelaces. Funny that I remember that.*

"Anything else."

The man had a long, jagged knife tucked inside his boot. Weird, but I've never had such vivid dreams before. It's as if I'm watching from behind him—like I'm there. Do you think it's my psyche trying to work through what happened to me?

He frowned. "Hard to say. Maybe. Can you remember anything else in this dream? A location? What the woman was wearing. Anything that could help pin this down?"

She sighed, then wrote, *Not that I can think of right*

now.

Reed tried to keep a level head with these dreams of hers. Yet, they could very likely be premonitions. Maybe her dying and being brought back had her tapping into something unexplainable. Either way, Taylor McClain had to be protected, and he was going to be the one to do that. She was too important to allow this killer to get to her again, especially if he learned that she might be seeing him committing these horrific acts in real-time. That would make her more than a liability. That would make her death a necessity, and Reed was going to see that didn't happen.

Chapter Seven

Taylor only felt safe when Detective Brentwood was around. He had an air of strength about him that suggested, *I could take down an ax murderer if I had to.* That made her want to be near him.

"I need to make a call. I'll be right back. Drink your coffee before it gets cold." He walked outside and closed the door.

Right away, Taylor wondered who he was calling and what it was about. She sipped her coffee, pacing the living room floor, her skin goose bumping.

As she was taking a seat on the sofa, he stepped back into the house, his expression unreadable. He came to sit in the chair across from her.

"So, we have a little problem, Taylor."

His words only intensified the bumps of her arms. On her tablet, she wrote, *What sort of problem?*

"Another woman was murdered tonight. I'm worried it's the same guy who attacked you, so you're going to need protection around the clock. My boss can't authorize it right now since we have a staff shortage. I know it's not the best solution, but I suggested that I'd do it on my off-duty hours until he could. Would that be all right with you?"

Would that be all right? Was he kidding? This was Taylor's best-case scenario. The one man who made her feel safe would be here to protect her. She was all in, and

56

then some.

She nodded, more than eager to have him stay.

"I need to check in at the precinct to grab my laptop and a file I need, then I'll pick up some things from my apartment. I should be back here in a few hours. Do you think you'll be okay until then?"

The hairs on her neck charged at knowing he was leaving. Yet, he'd be back. She nodded again.

"Maybe try to get some rest. Officer Stroop is outside. He's caffeinated and knows to be on the lookout for anyone suspicious. I'll return as soon as I can."

Taylor rose and walked him to the door.

"Lock up as soon as I leave."

He left, and Taylor sent the bolt lock home and secured the chain.

Sighing, she leaned against the wooden door, her mind reverting back to what Detective Brentwood had told her. Another woman had been killed. Was it the one from her dream? Was Taylor crazy to even think such a thing? Had something weird happened to her while she was unconscious? Why did it seem as if she had a strange mental connection to her attacker through these nightmares?

Stupid and insane, yes, but there was something happening here.

Taylor shoved away from the door. Her mind was conjuring up things that weren't true. These dreams had to be mere coincidence.

She needed to keep herself grounded. Perhaps working would help. The Trident account ad was due next Friday. She could get a jump on that and finish what she could. Then, if she wasn't ready to go back to the office, she could send it to her partner in crime, Adam, the one colleague and friend she trusted there, who could present it to them. This might be just the distraction she needed and would fill the time until the detective returned.

Taylor walked into the kitchen to get her laptop. She glanced out the window and saw the sun was starting to come up. *Good.* Daylight made her feel less vulnerable, more in control.

She sat down at the table and pulled up her file on Trident, in the corner of her computer, an email popped up into her inbox.

She clicked on the link and the words stopped her heart. DON'T THINK I'VE FORGOTTEN ABOUT YOU. CATCH YOU LATER!

XOXOXO

Her heartrate took off on a crazy acceleration and sweat formed on her upper lip. He was not going to leave her alone. He was going to try to get to her again.

Could he be outside right now?

She jumped up from the chair and raced to the front to look out the window. The police cruiser was still there, the officer inside popping something into mouth. At least he was awake, hopefully watching for trouble.

Why was this happening to *her*? If she hadn't gone to the gym that morning maybe her life would be normal. She should've listened to her friends and gotten her beauty sleep instead. All because of her vanity, wanting to look her best. Now, her face was a mess, and somebody was trying to kill her. Was he going to get to her? Would she die, like those women in her dreams?

She paced the living room again, her anxiety high. The more she thought about her impending fate, the more irrational she became. Her whole body started to perspire. She was trapped and wanted to get out of her condo, but she couldn't. Her attacker might be expecting her to do something stupid like that.

No. She was safer behind closed doors. Too bad she didn't feel like it.

How had this guy gotten her email address? Did that mean he also had her home address? He could very well be outside waiting for her to make the wrong move. Taylor wasn't going to oblige. She needed to keep her wits about her, not panic. Mistakes were made when you didn't think things through, and she refused to make this easier for him.

****

Reed stepped into the precinct's elevator, feeling like an idiot. So much for trying to keep his distance from Taylor. He was running headfirst into the lion's den, directly into the animal's mouth. How stupid was that? Too stupid for words, but it was a done deal, sanctioned by the chief, and too late to reevaluate now.

He pressed the sixth-floor button and blew out a ragged breath. When the doors opened, he ran straight into the two people he'd been avoiding—Sylvia's parents. It was early morning. Why were they here?

Her father didn't appear happy to see him. He looked as if he wanted to rip his head off. Could Reed blame him? Not really. He'd feel the same, if the roles were reversed and Richard had promised to find his daughter's killer with no success. The two had probably heard about the new murder and wanted to find out if there was any connection to Sylvia.

"I guess you haven't gotten our messages, Detective Brentwood," Richard said. "Why else wouldn't you have returned my calls?"

Talk about hitting him where it hurt—smack-dab in the gut. Getting kicked by a horse would have hurt less.

Shit. What could he say? The truth, perhaps.

"I was going to call you, Richard, but I was hoping to have something to tell you first."

"What's with these two other attacks? Are they related? Is it that same guy that killed our baby girl?" Richard's eyes became glassy, which only added to Reed's discomfort.

"We can't be sure yet, but there are some similarities in the cases. When I learn more, you will be the first to know. You have my word on that."

"You said that months ago. I'm not sure I can trust your word at this point."

The man questioning Reed's abilities to get to the truth and find their daughter's killer was like a knife to his stomach. He had to prove them wrong. "I know you're frustrated. I am too, but we will find her killer."

"What about this woman who survived her attack? Did she see him?"

Reed couldn't discuss other cases with them, but he could give the couple hope. "She didn't since he grabbed her from behind, but some forensics were found at the scene, unlike at Sylvia's. We are working on that now."

Richard nodded, placing an arm around his wife to comfort her. "Okay. We'll wait for your call, then."

Reed sighed. What he wouldn't give to have someone in custody for murdering their daughter, but at least he had some things to go on with the new cases. Unlike before. Sylvia's crime scene had zero evidence, nothing to lead them in any direction. But Taylor's had footprints and a possible suspect. The personal trainer at Taylor's gym. Now, he needed to see if the man had any connection to Sylvia or Jamie.

Reed watched the couple get on the elevator, then went to get the files on the new cases, and his laptop. He still had to go to his apartment, grab some clothes and toiletries before heading back to Taylor's. He wanted to get to her as soon as he could. For whatever reason, her troubling dreams only ramped up his sixth sense. The one thing that had always made him good at his job. Something that had drawn him to law enforcement in the first place.

With a feeling of urgency, he loaded everything he'd need into his duffle bag and started back toward the elevator. "Hey, Brentwood," someone shouted from behind him.

Reed turned to find Ken Vogel walking his way, a smirk on his face. "What's going on?"

"You'll be happy to know we found DNA under Jamie's nails and some clothing fibers that weren't from hers. She was strangled to death, then scalped. No signs of being raped. We're running the DNA we found against the DNA from Ms. McClain's attack. I should have that back by this afternoon."

This was good news. "Contact me as soon as you get it. If they're a match, then this guy is starting to get sloppy. What about footprints? Did your team find any?"

"Some deep tread prints, probably from a pair of boots."

Okay, that went along with Taylor's dream. This was starting to freak him out.

"Thanks for the information, Ken. I appreciate you putting a rush on this."

"I want this creep caught as badly as you do. This makes two women in less than a week. We must get this guy."

Reed nodded and pressed the down button on the elevator. "Let me know on the DNA."

"I sure will." Ken turned and walked away.

The doors opened and Reed got on. If the DNA matched, then they'd know they had one man responsible for the two attacks. And, if that were the case, Reed would gamble his paycheck that he'd killed Sylvia Moore as well. The cases were too similar not to be perpetrated by the same man.

Reed walked to his car with a spring in his step. Sylvia's attack and murder had been meticulous, the crime scene fiber- and DNA-free. Taylor's attack had been rushed. This sick fuck was becoming sloppy, and hopefully those slipups would be enough for Reed to catch him. Soon, before any other woman lost their life—especially if he planned to come back and finish the job with Taylor.

Chapter Eight

Taylor glanced at the time, suddenly realizing that if she hadn't been attacked, she would be getting ready for her best friend's rehearsal dinner right now. Tears clouded her eyes, and she gave in to her need to cry. She could almost see the joy on Camila's face. On Gavin's, her soon-to-be husband. This was another step for her and her best friend's life journeys, something they'd talked about for years. One or both of them getting married and starting families.

Taylor wasn't sure she was ready for that herself, but Camila couldn't wait to be a mother, and Gavin felt the same about having kids. Taylor was excited for them both.

She jumped at a knock at the door. Why couldn't she seem to calm down? This attack had changed everything.

Quickly, she went to answer as she wiped a stray tear from her eye. It had to be Detective Brentwood.

When she opened the door, he frowned. "Don't let anyone in before knowing who it is," he said in a stern tone. Then he walked inside and closed the door behind him.

He placed a duffle and another, larger bag down onto the floor then glanced at her. "Why does it look as if you've been crying? Did something happen while I was gone?"

"I was thinking that tomorrow is my best friend's

wedding, and I won't be there. It made me sad."

He stared at her, his eyes wide. "Wait. You're talking. How?"

"I thought it was time to try, and, well, it worked."

"Don't overdo it."

"I have to show you something." Taylor waved him into the kitchen, then brought up the email. "I got this about twenty minutes after you left."

He leaned in and read the note, his eyes widening again. "Shit."

"He's going to try and kill me, isn't he? Just like those other women."

"He's not going to be able to get to you, Taylor. I'll protect you."

Taylor knew what he said was true. If he was here, she'd be safe. But what would happen when he wasn't?

"First thing we need to do is find out who sent the email. I'm going to call and get someone working on that right now." He grabbed his phone from his breast pocket, pressed a number and waited. "Brad, I need help from your tech friend again. Ms. McClain got an email a few hours ago. We need to know who and where it came from." He looked at her. "I need your email address and password. After we get what we need, change the password."

Taylor wrote down what he requested and handed him the paper.

He relayed the info and ended the call. "They're going to put a rush on this. Hopefully, they'll have something in a few hours. Until then, try not to worry."

Easier said than done, but as long as the detective was there, she was safe.

"I'm sorry that you're missing your friend's

wedding," he said, grimacing.

"So am I. I should have listened to my girlfriends that morning and stayed home."

"Unfortunately, we don't know if this guy had been watching you for a while. You were lucky in a way since someone interrupted your attack. Another day or time, there might have been a different outcome. We just don't know."

Taylor hadn't thought of that. Now that it was in her head, her mind unraveled a realm of horrific scenarios. This guy could have broken into her home, murdered her, and no one would've known for days. And then, Camila would probably have been the one to find her. Something that she'd have had to live with for the rest of her life. No. It was better that it happened the way it did.

Taylor brushed the horrible thoughts away. One way or another, it wouldn't change anything. "Let me show you where you'll be sleeping. I'll warn you though, the bedroom is a bit girlie."

"I don't care about that. All I need is somewhere to lay my head. I could sleep on the couch if need be."

"There's no reason to do that. You'll also have your own bathroom. That was one of the reasons I bought the home. Guests have their privacy."

Taylor left the kitchen, Detective Brentwood following directly behind, stopping only long enough to pick up his bags.

She opened the door for him. "I'm going to warm up one of the meals my friends brought when I was at the hospital. I was shocked when I opened my refrigerator. I have enough for an army. You're welcome to join me. I'll call you when it's ready."

"Wait, Taylor. Are you saying that someone else has

a key to your place?"

"Yes. Camila, my best friend, has one. Why?"

His eyes narrowed. "Where does she keep it? I don't like the idea of anyone having a key to your house other than you. Is there a way to get it back until this guy is caught?"

Taylor shook her head. "She's leaving tomorrow night on her honeymoon and is probably on her way to her rehearsal dinner right now. I can't ask her to stop everything and bring me my key. I won't do it."

"Can you at least ask her to take it with her on her honeymoon?"

"Yes. I can text her now."

"All right. That will relieve my mind. There aren't any others, right? No hide-a-key anywhere?"

"No. I've never felt that was a safe option." Funny, she'd always been vigilant about that with her home, yet chose to walk out into the darkened parking lot alone. Seemingly dumb, but like the detective had said, maybe that act had saved her life.

****

Reed hated the idea there was a key to Taylor's home in someone else's hands, but what could he do other than change all the locks? That seemed a little extreme since it was one key, and her friend could take it with her.

Taylor left him alone in the bedroom, giving him a chance to look around. The color of the walls and bedspread was a soothing light green. The bed frame was a sleigh style, something he only knew about because his sister had the one their grandmother owned before her passing four years ago. She had been left the bed since she'd admired it every time she'd been to their grandmother's house.

A couple of hand-painted pictures hung on the walls, one of a lakefront landscape, a grove of fir trees off in the distance, a small, log-type cabin taking center stage. Picturesque for sure. The initials JAM was scrawled in the corner of the painting. Where was that picture done, and had Taylor been there?

He shook the thought and tossed his bag onto the bed, unzipping the top and pulling out his shaving kit bag. He took it to the bathroom, finding the sink with a glass bowl he'd only seen in magazines. The room was impeccable. Cleaner than any motel he'd ever stayed at. He placed his bag off to the side of the sink and returned to the bedroom, leaning down to test the mattress. It was one of those pillow tops. He was going to sleep like a baby tonight. His own mattress was hard and lumpy, probably why he didn't get much rest. Maybe it was time to invest in a new one.

He glanced around again, amazed. Nothing looked old, cheap or ordinary. How much money was there in advertising? Perhaps he should consider a new profession.

One thing was abundantly clear, though, Taylor McClain had great taste. Just then, she stepped back into the room, smiling at him. "Ready to eat? I warmed up a lasagna. And there's a blueberry cheesecake we can have for dessert. How does that sound?"

"Sounds great. I'll follow you."

As they made their way to the kitchen, Reed's gaze wandered to Taylor's nicely shaped behind in a pair of the sweatpants. *Damn. What are you doing, Brentwood? Get your eyes off the asset.* He was just tired and, frankly, hungry because he'd barely eaten since yesterday.

She'd set the table for two and had made a salad to go with the lasagna. With a spatula, she served him a portion and then gave herself one. "Would you like some wine or a beer? I don't have any manly stuff. Only micro-brews."

"A glass of water would be fine." Reed told himself he needed to stay sober and on full alert.

She brought them both glasses of water from her refrigerator dispenser, then took a seat opposite him.

Reed drowned his salad with ranch dressing, then dug in, pleased by the combination. He hadn't realized how hungry he was until she'd mentioned eating.

"How long have you been a cop?" Her question drew his attention away from his food.

"Almost ten years. I've been in homicide for a little over two." Reed was starting to enjoy the timbre of her voice, though he was sure the huskiness was amplified by the damage to her throat.

"How do you deal with murder every day?"

"To be honest, it's not easy. Most cops don't last long in our unit. Can I ask you a question now, Taylor?"

She smiled. "Of course."

"Have you ever had dreams like you told me about, before your attack?" This was something he'd been wondering since that morning. Was this new, or had she always experienced these types of dreams?

"No. Not ever." She shook her head. "I was wondering why this was suddenly happening to me. Why now? Was it something in my subconscious that's trying to make sense of the attack? I just don't know."

Reed got the feeling Dr. Jaipal had never told Taylor the extent of what had happened to her—that her heart had stopped twice. That she'd died and been brought back. He'd tell her if he thought it was his place to do so, but it wasn't—it was her doctor's.

Were these changes just while she was asleep? "Has anything else happened that was strange?"

She shrugged. "Not really. I just feel a connection with this guy now, like I'm inside him, watching what he's doing to these women."

For some reason, Reed believed her. Taylor seemed to have tapped into something with these dreams. Too bad she couldn't see the attacks happen before they did—she could save a woman's life, and a family years of heartbreak like Sylvia's and Jamie's. Yet that would make her a definite liability to the guy who attacked her. Which would make Reed's job even harder. It was a double-edged sword, one he and Taylor could both get hurt by if this killer learned of her new ability.

"It might be a good idea to keep a journal handy. If you have another dream like this, you could write everything down while it's still fresh in your mind. Every detail counts, no matter how insignificant it may seem."

"That's a good idea. I'll do that."

Reed spent the next ten minutes stuffing his face, then enjoyed the creamy cheesecake and coffee she served. He'd never enjoyed a meal so much, especially the company. Even with the yellowish bruising on her cheek, her busted lip, and the gash along her hairline, which was healing nicely, Taylor McClain was a strikingly beautiful woman. One who, under any other circumstance, wouldn't give him the time of day. Now, she was a captive audience, laughing at his silly jokes and stories that were a bit surly for polite society. But Reed was a cop, and that was all he knew.

"I better get this mess cleaned up, then maybe try to

get some rest. You look like you could use some yourself." She rose from the table, picked up some dishes and walked to the sink.

"Let me help you." He grabbed his dishes and joined her. Reed wasn't going to dwell on the fact she'd said he looked tired. His take was, *you look dreadful, like death warmed over.* He was sure he did. Probably the most unattractive man she'd ever spent time with.

He pushed the negative thought away and helped her load the dishwasher, his hand accidently brushing hers as they placed their glasses on the top rack. Their eyes met and held a moment, then she pulled back as if she'd been burned. Why would she find his touch tolerable? It wasn't like he was Adonis or even Mighty Mouse. Sure, he was tall, but this woman spent her free time at the gym, something he never did. Even if Reed had the time, he wouldn't work out. Other things took priority.

So, they were complete opposites, had zero in common, not to mention she was a crime victim in one of his cases. Legally, he couldn't have anything to do with her in that way, and he'd better keep reminding himself of that or he'd risk losing his job. Something he couldn't afford to do no matter how pretty and appealing she might seem.

Taylor McClain was off-limits and always would be.

Chapter Nine

Taylor woke with a start, her breathing labored, her heart thudding crazily in her chest. Still half-asleep, she reached for the tablet and pen on the nightstand. This dream had been different than the others. No murdered woman. No dark alleyway, and no blood. Yet, it was somehow more upsetting than her previous nightmares.

She felt disjointed in this one, like she was now the hooded man from her dreams, watching, waiting for something outside an unfamiliar place. It looked like a tavern, a neon sign in the window flashing *beer*. The storefront was rundown, in a shady part of town, metal bars on the inside of the large window and door. An older man stepped outside, his walk staggered, clearly drunk. He disappeared down the street, whistling a tune that faded off into the distance. Again her/his attention was fixated on that door. Every time it started to open, their heart rate would change, anticipation heightened, then disappointment hit when it wasn't the target.

Who were they waiting for? And why?

A siren went off behind them, and they jumped. It was time to leave or get caught. Now, they'd have to wait for another opportunity to get them.

This was where the dream ended for Taylor. So bizarre. She'd need to tell Detective Brentwood about it in the morning.

She glanced at the clock on the wall, lit by the hall

light she'd refused to turn off.

It was three a.m., too late to try to go back to sleep, yet much too early to wake the detective. She really should ask him his first name, though she did have his card. Did it have it written on it? She hadn't noticed.

He was incredibly handsome—something she never gave two thoughts to before that evening. There was something telling in his dark blue eyes, a warmth that spoke of a caring heart. Indeed, Detective Brentwood was a good, kind man. Why else would he offer to stay with her, a perfect stranger? He didn't have to. She was nobody to him, a victim of a crime he was investigating. Yet, he'd given her a sense of security by doing so. Taylor would never forget that.

The act alone drew her to him, made her look at him in a positive way and want to know more about him as a man. Did he have a girlfriend? A wife? Any children? She hadn't noticed if he wore a ring. She had been too wrapped up in herself. Pitying the fact that she wouldn't be going to her best friend's wedding. It was time to stop that now, especially after he'd suggested that things could have been so much worse for her—she could be dead like those other women.

She rose and walked to her bathroom. It was time to rip the bandage off and look at her face. Hiding from herself was childish. Taylor was a grown woman and needed to face her demons. Vanity was one of them. Now that she'd been given a second chance, it was time for her to look at life differently.

Taylor switched on the light, then stepped up closer to the mirror and took a ragged breath. She sighed as she stared at herself, impressed at whoever had stitched up her scalp. It was already healing, barely red, no doubt helped along by the antibiotics she'd been taking.

Her cheek was in the yellow stage of bruising, to the point that makeup would hide it. Her bottom lip had been busted open but not enough that it had needed sutures. All in all, she didn't look bad, way better than she'd imagined. So, all this hiding from the sight of her face had been completely unjustified—stupid really, and from now on, she planned to care less about her looks and more about becoming a better person. Perhaps, in some way, this experience would be a catalyst to growth for her, at least, that's how she was going to look at it for now.

She opened the shower door and turned on the water. She'd take a shower, get dressed, and wait for the detective to wake. Then she'd talk to him about her dream and see what he thought. The man had an analytical mind. Maybe he'd be able to figure out what it meant.

Once she'd showered, she sat at her vanity, staring at herself. Her hair was a tangled mess and dirty. But again, she wasn't going to let vanity affect her. When the stitches came out, she'd have something to look forward to, washing her hair—so simple and ordinary that she'd taken it for granted.

She smiled. From this day on, Taylor planned to enjoy every minute of every day now that she'd cheated death. Everything was going to be sweeter, extra vivid, more musical to her. Taylor was looking forward to her new view on life, as long as the man in the hoodie couldn't get to her again and end it before it began.

****

Reed rolled over and yawned, disoriented by his surroundings until he remembered he was at Taylor's house.

He reached over to grab his phone, shocked to find that it was seven o'clock in the morning. He'd gotten eight hours of sleep.

Shit. So much for protecting Taylor.

He shoved the blankets aside and yanked on his pants, angry with himself for having slept like the dead. Maybe not the best thought in this situation.

As he buttoned his shirt, a smell flooded the air around him. The aromatic scent of coffee and fried eggs had him walking straight to the kitchen where he found Taylor in front of the stove, her back to him. She wore a pair of tight-fitting jeans that molded to her body, highlighting her incredible behind.

So, that was what working out got you, a firm, perfectly shaped ass. *One a pair of hands could cup, and ....*

What the hell was wrong with him? This was completely unprofessional. Went against every rule he'd ever set for himself. Anyone linked to his cases was off-limits.

Pull it together, Brentwood. Stop looking at her in a sexual way.

He sucked in a breath and cleared his throat, loud enough that she turned her head, gracing him with a smile so alluring he almost bit his tongue. *Shit. Christ. Son of a bitch.*

"Good morning." She pointed to the coffee maker. "Cups are in the cabinet above."

Reed grabbed a mug and filled it to the rim, catching a subtle hint of a flowery scent that had to be Taylor. Hot to look at and smelled like something sweet and exotic. He was in deep trouble here, and he had no way out since he'd promised to keep her safe. But who was going to save him from this torture?

"I hope you like omelets. I don't have much here for breakfast."

"That's fine." Reed went to sit at the table, thinking distance would help. He took a sip of his coffee, refusing to look at her. He needed to focus on his job, one he'd lose if he even thought to take their relationship beyond her being *the victim* in a case.

When she brought him a plate, that overwhelming scent bombarded him once again and messed with his newfound reserve.

She brought herself a plate and a cup of coffee, then sat across from him, her seemingly happy demeanor changing. "I need to tell you about my dream last night. It was strange since I appeared to be looking through the hooded man's eyes this time."

Reed's mouth slackened. "What did you see?"

"Some rundown bar. He was watching the door. Clearly waiting for someone to come out. A siren close by scared him away."

"Was there anything about the place you saw that could identify it?"

"There was a flashing beer sign. And security bars on the door and window."

Probably half the bars in the city had flashing signs. That wasn't going to help, though the bars on the window and door might. It had to be a crime-ridden area of town. His side of the city. He knew it well. "Can you think of anything else? No matter how small or insignificant it might seem?"

She shook her head. "Not really. I wrote everything down that I could remember. That's pretty much it."

"No street sign, or anything with a name on it?"

She tapped at her lips, drawing his attention to them. *Stay focused. The sooner you catch this guy, the better.*

"There was a man that came out the door. He was staggering and whistled a tune as he left. One that was vaguely familiar. I'm sure it doesn't mean anything, though."

"You never know." She was probably right but maybe it could jar something else loose in her mind that she'd seen while watching him leave. Reed had learned early on in Homicide that the smallest of things could trigger recessed memory.

"Go back to when he stepped out the door. Can you see him?"

She closed her eyes. "I do. He's probably in his mid-fifties, slightly balding."

"How so. On top?"

"Yes. Definitely a receding hairline."

Reed smiled at her. "What about his face. Anything unusual?"

"His nose was big, bulbous with a lot of those broken, red veins."

"Okay. Good. What was he wearing? Do you remember?"

"He wore a tattered gray overcoat. I think a blue-and-white pin-striped shirt. Gray trousers."

"What was he whistling, Taylor? You hear the notes. One by one." To help her, Reed started to whistle. "What do you hear. Is it a song you recognize?"

She closed her eyes and started to hum, then her eyes popped open, and she said, " 'In a Different Light' by Doug Jones. I only know it because my mother had his album and played it all the time while I was growing up.

She was into old country music."

"Good. Now, listen while he's whistling the song. Is there anything you see?"

She closed her eyes again and started whistling the tune. "Yes. He walked by a dumpster that had Reemers on the side."

Reed smiled again. He now knew what area in the city they were in. Reemers serviced only downtown. That narrowed the search quite a bit.

"This helped a lot, Taylor. Maybe if you are up for taking a drive later, we can go look at some of the area bars and see if we can find this one. How does that sound?"

She nodded. "Sounds like a plan. I need to stay distracted today anyway since it's wedding day."

"Then we have a date." Reed wanted to kick himself for his suggestion. It was hardly a date, and yet again, he'd be with Taylor, in a closed car, alone. It was like he was trying to torment himself. But, if Taylor's dreams were becoming reality, they needed to find this place and learn why the hooded man was there. Was it someone who worked at the bar he was trying to get to? If that was a possibility, then Reed and Taylor needed to find out, no matter how hard it was on him.

Chapter Ten

Once again, Taylor glanced at the list of local bars Reed had given her. They had already visited two that were now crossed off and had ten to go. She'd had no idea how many taverns there were in the city until they'd had to find the one in her dream, and these were just the bars downtown. Apparently, people loved to drink.

"What's next?" Reed's question pulled her back to him.

"*James Tavern* on 112th street."

He nodded, then made a left turn at the light.

The street they entered was dirtier, more rundown, and made her want to lock her door. Was she being judgmental? Probably. People raised their families here too, loved their children as much as anywhere else.

"Have you worked down here?" Her eyes locked onto his profile. *Damn.* Just looking at him sent little shivers of excitement through her. Why had it taken so long to notice how incredibly handsome Reed Brentwood was?

"Homicides are common in this area, yes. Turf wars among gangs. Drive-by shootings. That type of thing."

Taylor sighed. "That's got to be sad for the people who live here."

He glanced at her, his eyes turning a warm denim shade. "It is. There are good people here trying to live their lives. Families trying to survive, and yet only the bad stuff gets talked about. It's so unfair. Areas like this need community action, better-paying jobs, and outlets for the youth. Then we'd have less recruitment from these gang members, who look for every opportunity to thrive. To do that, they need warm bodies—young and impressionable ones."

Reed seemed to know a lot about this lifestyle. Could he have come from an area such as this? Now she felt bad for having any negative thoughts. People needed help here, not recrimination.

He turned right at the next traffic light, onto 112th Street and parallel-parked in front of *James Tavern,* a storefront that instantly sparked her memories. "This is it. This is the bar he was watching. There's the Reemers dumpster." Taylor pointed toward the container, and her heart started to pound with excitement. This was the place. "Now what do we do?"

"We go in and find out why he was here?"

Taylor exited the car, waited for Reed to come around to her side, then they walked to the door.

Inside, loud country music pierced her eardrums and made her flinch. Staying here long would cause a person to go deaf. The tavern itself was dark and smelled of smoke, alcohol, and an old musty scent.

She followed Reed farther into the place. A handful of people were sitting on the stools next to the bar, a few in booths along the left side of the room. This was a first for Taylor. Being in a seedy tavern. Somewhere she would never have gone had the detective not been with her.

She glanced around at the people, who all seemed to be staring at them. Did they look so different? Like they didn't belong? Instantly, she felt like an outsider.

"Come on, let's talk to the bartender. See who was working last night."

The two seated themselves at the end of the bar, Reed shoving a bowl of shelled peanuts her way. How many hands had been touching those things? The thought made her squirm. She shoved them back toward him.

From behind the oblong bar, a tall African-American man walked over to them. "What can I get you two?"

"Give us two colas," Reed said without even asking if she wanted anything or not.

When the man left to get their order, Taylor frowned.

"You don't have to drink it. I need to get this guy to talk. Ordering something can only help."

The bartender returned and placed two dark sodas onto napkins in front of them. "Anything else?"

Reed paid the man, then took out his badge and flashed it his way, the bartender's dark eyes narrowing. "I have a few questions to ask you if you don't mind?"

The man's brows drew together. "About?"

"Can you tell me who was working here last night?"

"Angie was behind the bar. She works Friday and Saturday nights. Thelma was on the floor."

"So, will either of them be in soon, or am I going to have to come back?" Reed glanced at Taylor, who grimaced.

"Why do you need to talk to them? What did they do?"

"They didn't do anything. I simply need to speak with them."

The man's eyes narrowed again.

"Seriously, I'm just worried for their safety."

The man's dark-brown eyes widened. "Wow. Who is trying to hurt them?"

"I'm not at liberty to say. I just need to talk to both."

He glanced at the clock behind him, then turned back. "Angie should be in in twenty minutes for her shift. Thelma isn't due in until seven."

"Okay, thank you." Reed turned to smile at Taylor.

The thought of spending any more time there had her on edge, but what could they do? There had to be some reason the hooded guy was watching this bar, and if talking to Angie or Thelma saved one of their lives, then so be it.

While waiting, Taylor glanced around again, a man sitting in a booth catching her eye. He was pale as death and wore a hat that seemed out of another century. Hell, everything about him appeared dated. He sat there without even a drink in front of him. Weird for sure, and as she watched him, his attention swung her way. He stared back for the longest time, to the point Taylor had to look away. It was creepy.

She moved closer to Reed and a chill passed through her. When she glanced back, the man was no longer in the booth. She looked around the bar. Nope. He disappeared.

"Are you okay?" Reed asked.

Taylor wasn't sure. Not only was she dreaming about strange events, now she was seeing things that weren't there.

****

Reed wasn't sure what had happened with Taylor, but she looked white as a ghost. Maybe he needed to take her home. Perhaps their outing had been too much for her. After all, she had just survived a life and death situation.

"I'm all right." She gave him a bright smile. "I thought I saw something, that's all."

"Are you sure? I could take you home and come back to talk to these women."

"No. I'm fine."

Reed studied her for a moment, still concerned. She didn't look all right. But what could he do? She wanted to stay, and he needed to talk to these two. One of them had to be warned that someone might be watching them. But mainly, he wanted to see what they looked like since all the women who'd been attacked so far had similar features and hair color. If Angie or Thelma had the same, then she'd need a safety detail put on her to keep her out of the hands of this hooded killer.

"We could order a burger or something. Have you eaten anything since breakfast?"

"I'm fine." She refused to look at him. Something was bothering her.

The front door opened, and a woman in her late twenties walked in, her hair pulled up in a ponytail, the color hard to gauge, though the shape of her face was like Taylor's. *Shit.* This was just getting too weird for his liking. Taylor had clearly tapped into something with her dreams.

When the woman stepped behind the bar and drew closer, Reed could see her hair color and it almost matched Taylor's to a tee. This murderer had a type, and he'd need to contact Travis Sanders right away and talk to him about the profile.

"Hey, Ang," the bartender said. "The two at the end of the bar want to talk to you."

The woman looked at Reed, frowned, then with a

hesitant stride, walked over to them. "What do you need to see me about?" Her gaze moved to Taylor and her gray-blue eyes narrowed. "Do we know each other?"

Taylor shook her head, but also gawked at Angie, probably seeing the similarities too.

"I'm not sure if you've heard about the murders of those women lately or not, but that's why I'm here. I'm concerned that you fit this killer's profile and that you might be in danger."

Angie ignored Reed's comment and continued to gawk at Taylor. "What happened to your head?"

Taylor reached up and brushed at her stitches that were mostly hidden.

"I was attacked. He cut me and did this." She pulled down the turtleneck she wore to reveal the bruising on her throat.

Angie swallowed convulsively, her gaze shooting to Reed. "Why do I fit his profile? I don't get it."

"Taylor here was almost killed by him, and as you can tell, there are a lot of similarities between the two of you. I wanted you to be aware that you could be next."

"But how did you find me. I don't get it."

"I know this must come off as bizarre. I don't blame you for questioning it. I just want you to watch your back. Always have someone with you, especially when leaving the bar.

"But why me, or her, for that matter. I don't understand."

"I don't know why this guy has a type, but I promise to let you know when I find out. Until then, I'm going to see if I can't get you some protection."

"What kind of protection? I have to work, otherwise I'll lose my apartment. I'm already running behind on the rent."

"I'll see if we can't get you a uniformed office, who can stay outside your apartment door and the bar when you're here."

"Where are you from?" Angie asked Taylor. "I've never seen you here before, or around town."

"I live on Mandolin in Manchester."

"That's like another universe. How is this guy finding women who have similar looks from different parts of the area?"

Angie had a great question. How was this killer choosing woman that had the same characteristics? Facial recognition software perhaps? He clearly had computer knowledge because he could send emails that were impossible to track.

The more Reed thought about it, the more that seemed plausible. The killer knew programming and could have gotten his hands on some software that helped in his search. Maybe Brad's friend could help find this guy. Somehow, Vince Silva didn't appear smart enough to pull off this type of thing, though, Reed wouldn't count him out completely yet.

At this point, he had three people he needed to talk to before he took Taylor home. First, he had to get a beat cop down here to keep an eye on Angie twenty-four/seven, then he needed to call Ken to find out if the DNA on Taylor and Jamie had come back. Lastly, he had to call Travis to get him to come to town to profile these murders. Because this guy was stepping up his killing at a breakneck speed, and there had to be a reason why, one he needed to find out now before another woman was butchered.

Chapter Eleven

Taylor sat on the edge of her bed, gnawing on her bottom lip. Was she losing her mind? Seeing people who weren't there had to be a problem, one she couldn't simply chalk up to stress. Had something happened to her brain? Was it damaged from lack of oxygen? There had to be some reason why she was experiencing visions now. Perhaps she should talk to Dr. Jaipal and ask him if this couldn't be some temporary side effect to what she'd endured from her attack.

She heaved a sigh, wishing she could simply go back to life as usual.

What if that never happened? What if these strange aberrations continued? Maybe she'd end up in a psych ward, taking drugs to block them out. What kind of life would that be?

Taylor shook off the thought and stood, her stomach grumbling. She'd been brooding in her bedroom long enough. Time to buck it up and move forward.

She had no idea what Reed had been doing the last few hours, though she knew he was still there since he wasn't the quietest person. He was a big guy, and you could hear him walking around.

Determined not to feel sorry for herself any longer, she opened her door and stepped out into the hall, thinking about what she'd fix for dinner. As she reached the kitchen, she found Reed facing the window, his fists clenched at his side. Was there something wrong? Did she want to know if there was?

"Is everything okay?" she reluctantly asked.

He turned and gave her a weak smile. "I'm just angry that the chief refused to protect Angie without a reason other than she fit the profile of the killer we're hunting. He'd never understand about your dreams, and I can't be in two places at once."

"Didn't the bartender say he'd make sure she was safe."

Reed shook his head. "He doesn't know what he's up against. This guy is crazy. We don't know what he's capable of."

"Did you get a hold of your profiler friend?"

"Travis should be here by morning. He's working on the profile as we speak. He's the best in his field. Hopefully, we can get an idea of who this guy is and find him before anything else happens. I feel helpless right now. We're idly standing by waiting for this killer to strike again.

"Did your other friend find out who sent me that email?"

"That damned thing pinged all around the country. I'm beginning to think an email Sylvia Moore received that we thought came from some guy on a dating app was from the killer. We're going to need to go deeper, see where it was routed from. Whoever is doing this is a computer expert. Knows his way around IP rerouting. It could take weeks to learn where it originated from, and we don't have that kind of time."

"You're doing what you can, Reed. Why don't you sit down, and I'll warm up something to eat? Then we can put our heads together and come up with a direction to go in."

He nodded, then went to sit at the table and placed his phone on the top.

He was frustrated, and she couldn't blame him. But he was doing more than he knew. He was making her feel safe and she appreciated that now more than ever.

"Would it be all right"—she asked, while placing a casserole in the oven—"if I went by the hospital to talk to Dr. Jaipal tomorrow?"

His eyes widened at her request. "Is there something wrong? Do you need to go to the hospital now?"

"No, no, I'm fine. I just need to talk to him about something I've been experiencing. It's not a physical thing, Reed. So don't worry about that."

His blue eyes warmed a shade. "Is there anything I can do to help?"

"You already are. You're here and you make me feel safe. That helps more than anything."

There was something more with Reed as well. It wasn't just about her safety. He made her feel other things, but would he be receptive to those feelings? Could he be? Was there some rule that he couldn't get involved with a victim in a case? She had no idea, but it was something she should find out before she became even more attached to him.

She sat at the table with Reed, studying him closely—a man she could fall head over heels for if she didn't watch herself.

"I wanted to ask you a question."

"Okay, what's that?" He gave her his full attention.

"Were you brought up downtown? You seemed to know a lot about life for the people there."

His eyes widened at her question, shifting in his

chair.

"You don't have to tell me if you don't want to. I was just wondering."

"It's not that, Taylor. I'm just surprised that you picked up on that. Yes. I was raised downtown. My mother, sister, and I lived there after my father was killed."

"Oh, I'm so sorry. How did that happen?"

"He was a cop and was shot on a routine wellness check. Some guy was beating his wife and kids, and the neighbors' called the authorities. My father was the closest to the scene and was sent to check on the family. He didn't even get to the door before he was shot and killed."

Taylor's jaw slackened. What a tragedy for Reed to have had to endure. So unlike her own upbringing that had been charmed in comparison.

"That had to be so painful for you."

He shrugged. "I don't remember him. I was barely two at the time of his death. My older sister has more memories of our dad. My mother never really recovered from losing him. Never remarried. We lost her to cancer a few years ago. Right before she died, she smiled for the first time since his death. My sister believed that Dad was there to greet her as she passed and that's why she'd been so happy."

His reminiscences caused a strange flash of bright light to blind Taylor for a moment. Like she was recalling something she'd witnessed, but she couldn't quite figure out from what. Just one more thing she'd need to discuss with her doctor when she saw him tomorrow. Hopefully, he could make some sense of it all because it wasn't making any to her.

****

Reed had no idea why he'd told Taylor about his father's death. Even the people around him weren't privy to the details. Yet there was something about her that made him open up and reveal events from his childhood. Now, he was afraid if he stayed with her any longer, she might learn everything he'd hidden. All his deepest, darkest secrets—*one* only he knew about.

Why was he reliving that indiscretion now? He had more important things to worry about.

His phone rang. It was the coroner, and he answered with, "You got something for me, Ken?"

"I do. The DNA matched. Whoever attacked Ms. McClain, killed Jamie Denton."

He smiled. "Okay. So, anything on those fibers?"

"Yep. They were black and were a sweatshirt type material."

Like a black hoodie.

"Anything on the boot tread?"

"We narrowed it down to a Timberland boot. The tread from their brown, leather pair with black laces. Not cheap, so this guy isn't poor."

Again, Taylor was right on the money. Her dreams were more than they appeared. Could they be evidence?

How was she doing this? Maybe he'd need to talk to an expert in the field of ESP or life after death experiences. Because she had a gift, but was it limited to her attacker, or could it go beyond that? That was a million-dollar question that might only be answered in time.

"I appreciate you letting me know, Ken. Have a good evening."

"I will. You do the same."

Reed ended the call and stared at Taylor, who rose from her chair when the oven's timer went off. He watched her intently. What had her life been like before these dreams made her a conduit? Probably smooth sailing since she had nice shit. From her appliances in the kitchen, top-of-the-line in a shiny, stainless steel, down to her expensive-looking dishes and flatware. This woman lived a different life than Reed, and he'd better remember that. They were opposites in every way. Too bad that didn't stop him from being attracted to her. She stirred a fire deep inside him, yet her slightest touch could burn his career to the ground. Reed couldn't let that happen.

She returned to the table she'd set for two and placed a noodle, broccoli, and cheese casserole on the cooling mat and served them both a hefty portion.

Reed stayed focused on his food. Taylor was too tempting for her own good, and for his. He needed to keep her at arm's length and their interactions all about finding a killer and using her gift to do that.

The doorbell ringing had them looking at each other. "You stay here." Reed rose from the table, glad he had his firearm handy.

At the door, he glanced out the window off to its side, seeing a uniformed officer standing on the stoop. He quickly unlocked the door, wondering why the guy hadn't just called him.

"Hello. I'm Officer Andrews. Chief sent me over to keep an eye on Ms. McClain while you visit a crime scene."

The hairs on the back of Reed's neck charged. "What happened?"

An attack on another woman. She's alive but her

friend wasn't so lucky. A bartender at James tavern. He was stabbed to death."

Reed saw red. This was the chief's fault. That man would be alive now had he listened to him. "Was the woman's name Angie? Where is she?"

The officer looked at his notes. "Yeah, Angie Jasper. She's at Mercy Hospital downtown, along with another man who was also injured trying to save her."

What a fucking mess. All because the chief refused to put a protective detail on Angie. Now, one man was dead and two people were injured. Boy, was his boss going to hear about this from Reed.

He allowed the officer into the condo. "Don't let anyone into this house unless it's me. Understand? Tell Taylor I'll be back as soon as I can."

Reed stepped out the door, angrier than he'd ever been in his life. Another senseless murder and one that could have been prevented. That made him want to punch the chief's lights out, something that wouldn't help anyone and would only make him feel better for a brief moment anyway.

Chapter Twelve

Taylor woke, relieved not to have had another horrific nightmare. Last night, when Reed hadn't returned to the kitchen, she'd found a young officer standing in her living room. He'd informed her that Reed had to go, and he had no clue how long he'd be gone.

It had taken her hours to relax, then another to fall asleep.

She shoved her covers aside and rose, wondering what time Reed had returned. She walked to the bathroom, intent on taking a quick shower, then she planned to go to the kitchen to make coffee and wait for Reed to get up. For some reason, simply thinking about seeing him again made goose bumps ripple across her skin. What did that mean? That she was *into* him, that he made her feel things she hadn't experienced before. Hard to believe that her body would respond like this since her brutal attack.

After showering, she sprayed her hair with the dry shampoo that had been in the box on her stoop when they'd returned from James's tavern. It smelled like flowers, maybe a little too strong for her liking, but it made her hair look much better. In another week she'd get to wash it thoroughly, something she looked forward to.

She quickly dressed in a white cotton T-shirt and a pair of navy-blue leggings, then left her room and walked down the hallway, her mouth gaping as she passed the living room to find the officer asleep on her couch. So, Reed hadn't returned yet? Why?

Taylor walked to the kitchen to put on a pot of coffee, happy to see that it was daylight and looked to be a start to a beautiful day. The birds outside were singing, yet that didn't comfort her, not when Reed wasn't here. Had there been another murder? Taylor had no idea since the officer had refused to tell her anything. She'd been literally left in the dark.

When the coffee finished brewing, she grabbed a mug and filled it to the brim, then glanced at the clock on the wall. Camila was on her way to Bora Bora for the start of her weeklong honeymoon. She and her best friend had combed travel magazine after travel magazine to find the perfect destination. The Society Islands of French Polynesia was their final choice because of their warm, white sands and the Four Seasons resort that had huts with glass floors for the guests to watch fish swimming. A place Taylor would like to go someday herself—maybe on her own honeymoon. Reed popped back into her head. This man was becoming an obsession of hers, one that wasn't such a great idea. He might very well be off-limits to her.

A knock at the door made her jump. Was it Reed? She placed her mug down onto the counter and raced to the living room right as the officer was unlocking the door.

Reed entered, looking dreadful. Weary would have been a kind word for his appearance. "You can go," he said to the officer, who nodded and immediately left her condo.

She focused on Reed. "What happened?"

"He went after her, killed the bartender and stabbed another man trying to intervene. The bystander's in critical condition. Angie's a hysterical mess. Couldn't tell me anything that would help catch this guy. Doctors say she's blocking it out, and she may never remember. Hopefully, if the other man survives, he'll be able to tell us something, give us a description. If not, we're back to *fucking* square one."

Taylor couldn't believe this. They had spent time with both victims. It just felt so surreal. One minute someone was there, the next, they were gone.

"Let me go take a quick shower and change, then I'll take you to the hospital so you can talk to your doctor."

"Are you sure you are up for that?"

"Yes. I'll be fine, Taylor. I want you to see him if that's what you need to do."

Her heart clenched at his kindness. This man had been up all night and still cared about making sure she was happy. Why hadn't some woman snatched him up by now? He was a catch in her eyes.

He left her standing in the living room, feeling all these strange sensations. Maybe instead of seeing Dr. Jaipal, she should see a shrink.

She doused the thought and returned to the kitchen, to her now-cold coffee. Taylor stuck it into the microwave for a minute, an image of the young bartender bringing tears to her eyes. Reed had been right to worry. That man had no idea what he'd been up against and had not been prepared for an attack. A police presence would have probably deterred the killer, and that had to weigh heavy on Reed's mind. It was no doubt why he'd looked so defeated, and Taylor couldn't blame him. But it was hardly his fault. He'd tried to get a detail put on Angie.

The timer dinged and she grabbed her cup from the microwave and took a sip, almost burning her tongue.

Why had her life taken such a turn?

Her ringing doorbell brought her out of her wondering. Who could it be this time? Should she even answer it? Reed was probably still in the shower.

Taylor walked to the front door and glanced out the window where she found a tall, blond headed man, holding a folder in one arm. Reed had told her not to let anyone in she didn't know. "Who's there?" Her hand gripped the lacy curtain.

"I'm Travis Sanders. Is Reed here?"

Taylor released a breath and the curtain. *The profiler.*

With shaky fingers, she unlocked and opened the door, noticing right away the intense, silver eyes the man had. She'd never seen any like them before.

"Hello. Are you Taylor?" He gave her a warm smile.

"Yes. Come on in. Reed's taking a shower. He just returned from another crime scene."

The man's eyes narrowed. "Another woman was murdered?"

"No, but I'll let Reed tell you what happened. He should be out in a few minutes. Would you like some coffee while you wait?"

"I'd love some."

Back in the kitchen, Taylor poured him a mug. "Cream or sugar?"

"Black's fine, thanks."

She studied the man while he sipped his coffee. He wasn't as tall as Reed, not as sturdy, but handsome in his own right. His eyes alone were stunning. "How did you become a profiler?"

"I have a bachelor's degree in criminal justice and psychology, and graduate degree in forensic psychology. It seemed like the perfect fit for me."

"That's impressive. So, do you have any ideas about this killer?"

"A few. He clearly has a type he's targeting, which means to me that a woman from his past, resembling you and those other women, did something to hurt him, and he's evening the score."

"But that's crazy, isn't it?"

"Of course it is, but in his fractured mind he's doing what he needs to do."

"Which is what?"

"Rid himself of the woman who caused him pain."

She frowned. It didn't make sense to her, but she didn't study serial killers for a living. He did. And according to Reed, he was the best in the business.

"Travis." Reed stepped into the kitchen. "When did you get here?"

The man smiled. "Oh, about three sips of coffee ago."

Reed laughed and the sound sent an electrical charge through Taylor. She was becoming completely enamored with Reed Brentwood, and, unfortunately, it was too late to do anything about that.

****

Reed smiled when he saw Travis. Maybe he could make some sense of what drove this killer's need to make the mistakes he'd suddenly been making.

Taylor handed him a cup of coffee, one he needed and was grateful for.

"Did you come up with any theories?" Reed asked him, knowing that time was of the essence here.

Someone else could die if they didn't find this nut.

"First of all, I couldn't find any similar cases in any other cities. That suggests that his killing spree just started. To me that means, the subject of this guy's hate perhaps passed away without him getting his revenge. That's why he's transferring it to women who resemble her, what she looked like when his mind was first fractured. Probably the man's mother or perhaps a grandmother."

"But why is he taking pieces of these women?" Taylor gasped.

Shit. Reed had forgotten she didn't know the specifics of the other cases. He glanced at her and wanted to kick himself. She looked pale and horrified. "Maybe you should wait in the living room, Taylor? This could get graphic."

"No," she shot back. "I need to hear what I'm up against and now my dreams are making more sense."

Reed respected her bravado, but he could tell it was all an act. She was putting on a brave face. Inside, she was scared as hell.

"What's this about dreams?" Travis raised a brow.

"She's had some dreams about the women who have died, depicting their murders almost to a tee."

The profiler's eyes widened. "Seriously? When did this start?"

Taylor looked at Reed, who said, "Tell him. He needs to know everything."

She nodded. "They started right after my attack."

"Wow." He looked at Reed.

"Let's put that away for now and get back to this killer. Why is he mutilating his victims?"

Travis shifted from one foot to the other. "The body

parts thing is not all that uncommon. We can go back to movies. *Put the lotion on the skin*, kind of thing. But I'm thinking it's something else with this guy. One theory I have is that he's obsessed with rebuilding the woman he hates. His need to get even is so great that he must reanimate her to do so, and like I said, this is just my first theory."

The mere idea sickened Reed. "That's some crazy shit."

Travis nodded. "Another idea was that perhaps he's reliving something this woman had done to him as a child. He's reenacting the event onto these women and taking it a step further by killing them. Until I can really dig into the case files, I'm going to go with these two scenarios and work up a profile from them."

"I have all the files you'll need here, so if you are up to it, you can get started now. I'm going to take Taylor to an appointment this morning. We can talk when you've had a chance to go over the files."

"Sounds like a plan. I need to check in to the motel I reserved anyway, then I'll dig into the material. Maybe we can have dinner together and go over what I came up with."

"That sounds good." Reed glanced at Taylor, who nodded in agreement.

Reed rounded up the files for Travis, then led him to the door and said his goodbyes.

"You ready to go to the hospital?" he asked her.

"I just need to grab my purse and a sweater. Then we can go."

Reed watched her walk down the hall, the pants she wore molding like a second skin to her behind. *Dammit all to hell, Taylor. Do you have to dress like that? It's too hard to ignore.*

Reed sucked in a breath, refocusing his attention on his shoes. Best to keep his eyes away from temptation. Everything important depended on it.

She returned in a bulky, blue-and-white striped sweater, one that hid all her sexy curves. *Thank the good lord Jesus.*

"Ready?" he asked.

"I am."

On the trip to the hospital, Reed kept his eyes on the road. Looking at her didn't help him reevaluate what he needed to keep in the forefront of his mind. He knew both men who'd been involved in the attack last night had been transferred to Holy Trinity, though Ab Bradley, the bartender, had died fifteen minutes after he'd arrived and was probably in the basement morgue right now. Sam Evens, the man who had stepped in to help, was still in critical condition the last Reed had checked. While Taylor was seeing Dr. Jaipal, he'd go check on Mr. Evens, and Angie who was there under a psychological evaluation. She had non-threatening injuries, but her hysterical outburst had them sending her to Holy Trinity to get her emotional state under control. Reed could understand why after learning Angie and Ab had been dating.

In the parking garage he was lucky to find a free spot on the ground level. They stepped into the hospital and checked in at the information center. The doctor was currently en route and would meet Taylor on the sixth floor, and they'd talk in the office he used when he was there.

Reed planned to wait until he came, then go look in on Angie and Mr. Evens while she was with the doctor.

He didn't want her left alone for even a minute.

On the floor, they went to sit in the waiting room. "Are you doing all right?" He knew that what he and Travis had talked about earlier had to have influenced her.

She shrugged. "At least now I understand more aspects of my dreams. All the blood. The container with ice. He was putting these parts in it. What kind of a man is capable of that?"

"You'd be surprised, Taylor. I see the worst of society. It's not pretty."

"This guy would have taken a part of me if someone hadn't come along. With the cut on my scalp, I can guess which."

"Try not to think about that. You're safe and I'll keep you that way." Reed's promise to her was just that, a promise he'd keep if it meant losing his own life. Hopefully, it wouldn't come to that, and they'd arrest this guy before he had a chance to get to anyone else and destroy yet another family's life.

Chapter Thirteen

Taylor clasped her hands together, too nervous to sit still.

Dr. Jaipal gave her a bright, reassuring smile. "So, Taylor, tell me what you've been experiencing?"

When she didn't respond, he continued, "Anything you tell me will be strictly confidential."

"First, I'd like to know the extent of what happened to me."

The doctor shifted in his chair. "Are you sure you want to know that?"

Why wouldn't she? What was he hiding?

"Yes, I do."

He cleared his throat, making her catch her breath.

"Please just tell me."

"All right. You were revived on the scene by paramedics, and your vitals remained unstable. When you got here, you coded again. It took us a while to bring you back."

Taylor sucked in a breath. "So, what you're saying is that I died, and you revived me?"

He nodded. "Yes. It was a miracle how fast you turned around after that. I was concerned that you could have had lasting damage."

"You mean to my brain?"

"Yes, but everything looks fine."

Yet she wasn't fine. She saw things that weren't

there. "Actually, I think I *am* having problems."

His dark eyes narrowed. "What kind of problems?"

"I'm seeing people who are there one minute, then gone the next, and my horrific dreams are coming true."

His eyes narrowed even further. "How do you mean?"

"The last one I had was as if I was seeing through my attacker's eyes. Before that, I dreamed of two women being murdered, one killed months prior to my attack, and the other having just happened. Am I crazy? What's going on with me?"

"I'm not sure, Taylor. Your MRI showed no signs of damage. We could run a few more tests, but I'm not sure it would reveal anything."

Taylor wasn't sure what to say. Maybe she was losing her mind.

"How about you let me do some research on aftereffects of life-after-death experiences, and I'll call you. Meanwhile, I can put you on a mild sedative that could help."

He wanted to put her on a drug. That was the last thing she needed. She shook her head. "I'll be okay. Maybe it's just stress."

He smiled again. "That could very well be the case. Try to stay calm, and I'll do some research, and if you change your mind on that script, I can call one in for you."

Taylor nodded, only to appease the doctor. This wasn't stress; it was something much more ominous.

She rose from her chair. "Thank you for your time, Dr. Jaipal." Right now, she needed to clear her head, get a handle on the fact that she had been dead for some time, then brought back.

Taylor had read articles about people who had woken after a life-and-death experience and had been able to see things. Maybe that's what was happening with her. The question was, would it last?

Who was the man in James Tavern? An aberration? An actual ghost? Why was he at the bar? Had he died there? Was that how it worked?

In half a daze, Taylor left the doctor's office. She wasn't ready to face Reed yet. He'd probably think she was a freak.

She took the elevator down to the ground floor and stepped through a pair of doors, not caring where it led her. As she came around a corner, a cold chill raced through her. "Hey, I know you," someone said from behind her.

Taylor turned and her jaw dropped, the hairs on her arms and neck charging. It was the bartender from James Tavern. But it couldn't be. She was imagining things again. He wasn't there. It was all in her head.

"Where am I?" he asked, his whole demeanor tense, his eyes wide. "Where is Angie?"

Oh, my God. It had to be him. Why else would he mention Angie?

"Please tell me?" His eyes were sad, and Taylor's heart wrenched.

"You're at Holy Trinity Hospital. I don't know where Angie is, sorry."

"Where do I go? I've been wandering around for hours now. No one will talk to me. You are the first to even acknowledge I exist."

"You don't remember what happened?"

He shook his head. "Angie and I were leaving the bar together. That's the last memory I have."

Taylor contemplated what to say when someone else called her name. She turned away from the man as Reed came toward her, his feature drawn. "Why didn't you call me when you finished talking with the doctor?"

"I needed time to think." She turned back and sighed when finding the bartender gone.

"Can I ask you not to go off by yourself again? It's not safe, Taylor."

Should she tell Reed what she'd seen? How had the man ended up here in the first place? There were hospitals downtown. He wouldn't have been taken here. Did that mean that what she saw wasn't real? Maybe she was losing her mind.

"Are you okay? You look pale. Was the doctor able to help?"

Right. Not as pale as the man she'd just been talking to. Then again, he'd been dead.

"I'm fine," she lied. "Can we go home now?"

He stared at her intently, then nodded. "Of course."

On the way home, Taylor played over what the doctor had told her, then the event with the bartender. Jaipal said she had no brain damage. So, it wasn't that. That flash of light she'd experienced yesterday came back into play. Perhaps that was the bright light that people talked about when they passed. The so-called afterlife. When she returned home, she'd need to do some research. Try to find someone who knew more about these types of events, help her try to find a way to deal with them, because right now, she wasn't sure she could.

****

Reed allowed Taylor to step inside, then followed her into the condo and locked the door. He was exhausted, but she was troubled by something. He hoped he'd be able to get her to talk about whatever it was and then try to reassure her that everything would be all right.

"I have work to do." Her comment drew his attention to her. "I'm going to my room. You were up all night. You might want to get some rest."

She turned and left him standing alone in the living room. What was bothering her? He hadn't known Taylor long, but he could tell when something was off, and there was something she wasn't telling him.

Instead of going to the spare room, he walked to the sofa and sat down. With the murder and mayhem from last night, he couldn't sleep for any length of time. That pillow top mattress was much too comfortable. The hard sofa would guarantee him less sleep. He just needed to close his eyes for a few minutes and catch his second wind to get through the rest of the day and dinner with Travis tonight.

Reed shrugged off his blazer and threw it over the arm then laid his head back. As he closed his eyes, crying from down the hall sent his heart into his throat. Something had to be seriously wrong with Taylor, but should he go find out what? Would she be angry if he did? Reed didn't know what to do. He never was good with a woman in tears. Always seemed to make the situation worse. *Just block it out, Brentwood.*

Reed squeezed his eyes closed again, which seemed to amplify the crying. *Jesus Christ. Do something.*

He rose and took off down the hall, knocking lightly at the door. When she didn't answer, he opened it, finding Taylor lying on the bed, her face blotchy, a hand wiping at her tears.

Reed stepped closer to the bed. "What's wrong,

Taylor?"

She turned toward him, her eyes brimming with unshed tears. Seeing her like this cut him deep. "Tell me what's upset you?"

"I think I'm going crazy?"

Her confession was the last thing he'd ever imagined her saying. "Why do you think that?"

She shook her head. "I'm seeing strange things that can't be there."

"Such as?"

"People."

Reed didn't know what to say. "Who are these people you're seeing?"

"There was a man in James Tavern the other day. He was there one minute, then he was gone."

"So that's what had caused you to get upset? You saw this guy?"

She nodded.

"Okay. You said people. Who else have you seen?"

She sniffed and wiped her eyes again. "The bartender was at the hospital today. But you told me he was dead. So, it couldn't have been him, right? The only thing that shocked me was he asked about Angie. See, I'm bonkers. Crazy. Nuts. Losing my sanity, right?"

Reed's jaw slackened. Taylor didn't know that Ab Bradley, the bartender, died at that hospital. How could she?

"Did the doctor tell you the extent of what happened to you, today?" To go any deeper into this discussion Reed needed to know what she'd learned.

She sat up in bed and sighed. "He told me I died, and they brought me back. I'm starting to wonder if I wouldn't have been better off if they hadn't."

"Don't say that, Taylor. You are very lucky to be alive. Whatever you are experiencing now, you'll learn to deal with in time."

"So, you don't think I'm crazy?"

"Not at all. I think you were given a second chance, along with a new gift. One that neither of us understand right now. The man you saw today, Ab Bradley did die at Holy Trinity. He was transferred there from a downtown hospital, thinking he'd have a better chance of survival. But they got him there too late. Angie is also there, in the psychiatric ward because they don't have one downtown."

"He was looking for her. You don't think he'll haunt her…?"

"I hope not. She's struggling already with what happened. That's why she's there."

"So, you don't think it's crazy that I'm seeing dead people?"

"There are so many unexplained things in life, Taylor. I think we need to get in contact with someone who knows more than I do about these kinds of phenomena."

She pointed to her laptop. "I was trying to do that before I let my emotions get the better of me."

"Did you find anything?"

She shook her head. "Tears blurred my vision."

"Let's do it together." Reed smiled.

She reached for the laptop and patted the mattress beside her. Reed hesitated a moment, then plopped down next to her as she typed in "seeing ghosts after a near-death experience." Hundreds of links came up.

"Definitely more than I thought there would be," he said, reading some of the headers.

She clicked the first, finding it was a man who'd been clinically dead for ten minutes.

"Did Jaipal tell you how long you were gone?"

"He said it took a while to bring me back."

"I think we need to narrow the search to anyone from this area. That way we could actually go talk to them."

"We could do that?"

"If it will help you, Taylor. I'm willing to do it."

She smiled and Reed, suddenly realized how inappropriate it was for him to be next to her in bed. Heat infused his body and charged the air around him.

Shit.

"You keep looking. I'm going to go make us some coffee. I'll be right back."

Reed rushed from the room, in no hurry to return. If he didn't watch himself, he was going to do something stupid, like kiss her, which would lead to more. And that could very likely get him fired from his job—something that had taken complete focus of his life the last ten years. He couldn't allow anything or anybody to change that.

Chapter Fourteen

Taylor allowed Reed to open the door for her, then stepped into the restaurant, glancing around the room. She spotted Travis sitting at a table in the back. He waved them over. She was still confused about Reed's abruptness earlier, though their chemistry was undeniable. His eyes had warmed to a chambray blue, and a sexual awareness had surrounded them both, making it hard for her to breathe. Maybe he'd realized where things were heading and had second thoughts, and that's why he'd returned with only one cup of coffee for her, then told her he needed to get some rest before their meeting.

Reed held out a chair for her and she sat, not sure why she was even here. She was sure, if given the chance, Reed would have come alone. Too bad he felt responsible for keeping her safe.

He took the seat next to hers and then picked up the menu. Taylor did the same, not feeling at all hungry. She was too anxious to eat.

A blonde waitress stepped over to their table.

"Are you ready to order?" She had her pencil posed to write.

Reed and Travis looked at Taylor, who again glanced at her choices. "I'll have the Caesar salad with Italian dressing on the side."

"Anything to drink?"

"A glass of water, please."

Both Reed and Travis ordered steak and baked potatoes. Coffee to drink.

Once the waitress had gone, Taylor twisted her napkin between her fingers, wishing she was anywhere but there.

"Did you manage to work up a profile for this killer?" Reed asked.

Travis sighed. "I did." He pulled out a sheet of paper and glanced at it. "From my assessment, the man is probably in his mid to late forties. Both parents' dead. Either his mother or grandmother abused him as a child. Not sure about sexual abuse. That's hard to say since these women he attacked weren't raped. Not sure he's in the system because of this abuse. I think it was probably hidden from the people around him. He's well liked in his community, an accomplished man who has this hatred of *one woman* who these women resemble."

Taylor's jaw dropped and her eyes widened at the fact that Travis Sanders could come up with such a detailed profile from just studying the scenes and women this person killed.

"Do you think there was any sign of this man's fractured mind before he attacked his first victim?" Reed asked, glancing at Taylor, then looking back at his colleague.

Travis frowned. "Probably."

"We weren't lucky with the two murder scenes, besides getting DNA and some clothing fiber. But we do have boot prints in a size eleven. We also have a handful of possibilities with Taylor's attack. There were several men at the gym where she'd been working out that morning. I can get you a rundown on them. See who might fit that profile.

"Thanks. That would help a lot."

"Most of that is in my car. Remind me to give you my notebook before we leave."

The food arrived and Taylor pushed the salad around on her plate. All this talk about the killer caused her stomach to churn. She wanted to go home, curl into bed, and just forget about the last week. She wished she could go back to the carefree life she'd had before her dreams turned into nightmares and her days weren't filled with people popping in and out like a magic trick. Too bad that wasn't going to happen, unless maybe she went to see someone who could help her deal with this new gift or curse. A shrink perhaps.

Reed brushed her arm. "You're not eating. Are you okay?"

She gave him a weak smile. "Just tired. That's all." She then took a bite of her salad to placate him. She was fighting the tingling sensation that had gripped her when he'd touched her arm. The man had become an electric current on a live, exposed wire and it was unnerving to say the least.

Reed's phone rang and he reached into his jacket to answer it. "Brentwood. That's great. I'll come by in the morning to talk to him. The detail is still there, right? Okay. See you tomorrow."

Taylor studied him, waiting for Reed to tell her who it was, but he didn't seem in a hurry to do so.

"What was that about?" she asked, realizing he wasn't going to say anything.

"Maybe it's best for you to not know, Taylor. This is police business, and it should stay that way."

She was completely taken aback by his one-eighty

turn. It was dizzying. Before this call, he was keeping her in the loop, and now suddenly, he was being evasive. Why the sudden change? Did she do something to cause it? Whatever the reason, his abruptness hurt. It was like he was trying to push her away, and if Travis wasn't there, she'd ask him if that were the case. But he was, and if this was what Reed wanted, to keep everything cop/victim then that's what he'd get from her as well.

She dug her phone from her purse and found Camila's number. She'd spend the rest of the meal texting to find out how her honeymoon was going and ignore both men.

An hour later, they were on their way back to the condo, her mood so much better since she'd texted her best friend. Camila could always brighten any dark day, no matter the issue. Taylor was going to push everything away for now and focus on her best friend getting back and them working on her new house. That would keep Taylor from thinking about Reed and his new attitude toward her.

****

Reed knew Taylor was angry with him, but that was for the best. Being near her was getting harder for him. Her keeping her distance would be much less so.

He pulled into the driveway, and she practically jumped from the car, not bothering to stop once she'd opened the door. He was barely out of the driver's side when she slammed it behind her. Yep. She was pissed.

With a heavy sign, Reed walked up the stoop and entered the house, securing the lock and chain, glancing around. Taylor was gone.

He checked the kitchen, but she wasn't there. So, she was probably in her room for the night, intent on not dealing with him until morning—if then.

He'd have to talk to her sometime, especially since he was going to have to leave her with another officer in the morning. The man stabbed in the last attack had made it through surgery and had regained consciousness. Reed had to go to the hospital and interview him. Hopefully, he'd be able to give him a description of the man responsible for all these murders.

Reed made his way to the spare room. He might as well try to get some sleep since he'd only managed a few hours earlier on the sofa.

He sat down onto the mattress and untied his shoes, pulled them off and placed them beneath the bed.

His jacket ended up over the foot of the sleigh, along with his holstered gun, shirt and pants. He laid back on the pillow, his arm behind his head, staring up at the ceiling, angry with himself for not handling the situation better with Taylor. He simply wasn't good at this kind of thing. As far as he was concerned, women were from another planet. He didn't understand what made them tick, and probably never would. Growing up, his mother's reaction to everything made it impossible for him to feel sympathy. She'd been like an empty shell after his father's death, and he was too young to remember how she was before that. So, this whole thing with Taylor made him confused and uncomfortable.

He rolled to his side, studying the picture on the wall. Who had painted the scenic view since it wasn't a replica but an actual oil painting?

A thud from somewhere had him sitting up straight. Where had it come from? He rose and jumped into his pants, unholstering his gun. He stalked to the door and eased it open, listening intently. He didn't hear anything.

Cautiously, he slid down the wall to the living room. Nothing seemed out of place. He continued into the kitchen, every nerve in his body tense, the hairs on the back of his neck charged.

Another bump came from the opposite end of the house. Maybe it was just Taylor doing something in her room. He started back toward the hallway, then hesitated outside her door. He didn't want to go in if he didn't have to. He leaned closer to listen, his heartbeat thumping in his ears, making it harder to discern if she was awake or not. Maybe if he just took a quick look inside, he'd be able to ease his mind. He turned the knob and pushed the door open, spotting Taylor in bed, asleep.

He shut the door and started back toward the spare room. Perhaps it was nothing since it hadn't woken her up. Houses often made noises. He'd entered the room when a loud thud had him turning around again. Where was the sound coming from? He walked back to Taylor's room, thinking he'd wait for the noise this time. Her door flew open, and she screamed, only covering her mouth when she realized it was him.

"Did you hear that bump?" she asked, then her eyes widened. Reed hadn't put his shirt on, and she'd noticed.

"I did hear it. I can't figure out where it came from."

"It happened a few nights ago as well. The same night I had the dream about that second woman being strangled."

"Why didn't you tell me about it?"

"I just thought I was being paranoid."

"Let me get past you to look out your window. It sounds like something is bumping the side of your condo."

His suggestion made her face pale, yet she moved to

let him by.

Reed went to the window and peered out, looking closely at everything, watching for any type of moment.

Taylor came up behind him, so close he could feel the heat of her body on his back. "See anything?" Her breath was next to his ear, her voice barely above a whisper. Her nearness sent a charge through him, the pit of his gut clenching tight.

He sidestepped her, needing distance. "If something was out there, it isn't now.

"Are you sure?"

"Yeah. I think it might have been an animal or something. You don't have a trashcan out there, do you?"

Taylor shook her head. "No. That's in the garage."

He wished he could be sure that the noise hadn't been *someone* lurking outside, but he couldn't. He checked the locks on the window, relieved they were good quality construction. It'd be hard to pry one of the windows open, and if they tried to break the glass, he'd be in there before anyone could get to Taylor.

"Well, I think we should both try to go back to bed. I'll look in the back in the morning, see if there are any tracks. Goodnight."

Reed walked to the door. It was hard to be around her, especially in the skimpy tee and shorts she wore. The woman had legs that went on forever and looking at them stirred a certain body part, one that wasn't allowed to come out to play.

He closed her door, went back to the spare room, and sat down on the mattress, trying to calm his raging libido. Maybe it was time to find out if they had another officer who could stay with her since he wasn't handling this situation well. Neither was his body, and that alone could lead to him doing something stupid. Then he'd lose his job—a life-altering event that could not happen.

Chapter Fifteen

Taylor rolled over again, too pent up to sleep. Every time she closed her eyes, she saw Reed, shirtless, surprisingly fit for a man who barely had time to sleep. He had damned nice abs, arms, and a firm chest, all sprinkled with coarse, dark hair. She was lucky her jaw hadn't dropped open and spittle hadn't dripped out of her mouth in front of him. Even now, her fingertips tingled simply thinking about running them over every inch of his body. Yet, he wasn't into her. That was clear now since he'd had an opportunity to act on their attraction and he'd simply gotten up and walked away. Their connection wasn't strong enough for him. She needed to remember that from this day forward, and she had more pride than to throw herself at him. He'd no doubt rebuff her advances, and that would be devastating.

She punched her pillow, trying to get comfortable, hoping that would help her nod off.

She closed her eyes and there he was again, tall, lean, and sexy as hell.

Taylor slammed her fists into mattress and sat up straight. This was crazy. The man causing her restlessness was probably sound asleep, dreaming sweet dreams. Something she hadn't been able to do since her attack.

She rose and padded to her bathroom, thinking of taking something to help her sleep. Melatonin would work and it wouldn't cause her drowsiness in the morning.

In the cabinet she grabbed the bottle, and opened the top, popping a pill into her mouth. Then she ran water into the cup on the sink and swallowed. Maybe now she'd be able to rest. She returned to bed and lay there staring at the ceiling, imagining sheep jumping over a round bale of hay—something her mother had taught her when she was young. It'd always worked then. Hopefully, it would now. Ninety sheep in, her eyes became heavy, and she closed them.

It was dark but off in the distance a light shone through a window. With each step, it got brighter and started to come into focus. A fence gate seemed to slow things for a moment, then it came open and the movement continued. The building's window seemed familiar. A ninety-degree expanse of the perimeter only reaffirmed that and sent a chill through her. It was the back of her condo. So why was she being shown this? What was going on. Suddenly, she saw her bedroom window, hands reaching out, their fingers digging under the sill. Were they trying to open it to get in? The curtains inside had a gap, an inch or two in width, wide enough to catch a glimpse inside the room. What she saw startled her awake, her attention riveted to that window where she saw someone's eye looking in at her.

Taylor screamed.

She heard a door open, then footsteps coming down the hall. Her door flew open, and Reed came rushing in, this time shirt- and pant-less, a gun clutched in his hands.

Taylor pointed toward the window. He raced over and pulled the curtains open and looked out, his eyes widening.

He raced from the room, and she could hear him talking to somebody. When he returned, his whole face was masked with concern.

"I saw someone in black take off through the back gate. If it's who I think it is, you aren't safe here any longer. Pack a bag. We'll go stay at my place tonight until I can get a safe house put in place for you."

Taylor didn't want to leave her home, but what else could she do? She was still grasping the fact that she'd dreamed the whole thing. She'd save that little nugget of information for later, when she had time to replay it all in her head.

She walked to her closet and reached up for her largest overnight bag, pulling it down. Without thinking, she started stuffing it full of clothes, not caring that they'd all end up with wrinkles. In the bathroom, she retrieved her makeup bag and filled it with essentials.

She placed it in the large bag and went to get her laptop. Reed waited in the living room, looking up from his phone as she entered. He was dressed and wore a worried look.

"You ready?"

"I think so."

"If you forgot something, I could come and get it once you are placed in a safe house."

"Can't I just stay with you until you catch this guy?"

"I have a job, Taylor. I can't watch you all day."

Taylor recoiled at his biting words. Somehow things had changed between them, and it felt like a kick in the gut.

She walked to the door, determined to put an emotional distance between her and Reed from that moment on. If he was going to be cool to her, she'd do the same.

The ride to his apartment was so quiet, she could hear her heart beating.

He pulled into a complex twenty minutes later. Reed's apartment was on the second floor, not accessible from the outside. Taylor stood behind him, clutching her bag, wanting to bolt in the opposite direction. Inside, she glanced around, finding it so unlike her own place. Stark white walls. Minimal furnishings. "You'll be staying in my bedroom. I'll sleep on the couch."

"I hate to do that to you." Taylor felt bad about putting him out.

"I sleep on the couch half the time anyway. So, don't worry about it. Hopefully, in a day or two, we'll have another place for you to stay. I know mine isn't all that appealing."

"It's fine."

"Put your bags down and I'll go place some clean sheets on the bed."

"Let me help," she said, too anxious to stay put. This whole thing caused her anxiety, yet before Reed became distant toward her, she could deal with it. Now, it just made her want to run away and hide. It wasn't like she didn't have somewhere she could go—somewhere her attacker wouldn't be able to find her. That might be an option if things got more tense between her and Reed.

She followed him toward the back of the apartment, determined to appear unfazed by his cool demeanor.

In his room, she found the furnishings sparse, nothing on the walls. Just a bed, nightstand and a three-drawer dresser. It was like he'd just moved in, yet she'd bet that wasn't the case. The place was like the man—distant and suddenly cold as ice.

****

Reed hated how things had gone with him and Taylor, but he couldn't get close to her. She was too tempting. Too desirable, and there was something going on in her head that she was keeping close to her vest. Could he blame her, though, since his frostiness today?

"Are you hungry?" He hoped that eating would somehow help cut through the tension.

"No but go ahead if that's what you want." She refused to look at him, which only made him feel worse. He shouldn't have snapped at her about having a job to do. He should've tried to explain without making her feel like a burden. Unfortunately, he couldn't take it back now no matter how much he'd like to.

"You really should eat something, Taylor."

She shook her head. "I'm tired. Would you mind if I go to bed?"

"No. Not at all." Reed turned to leave, closing the door behind him. Maybe some sleep would help them both. He retrieved a pillow and blanket from the hall closet and walked to the sofa to sit down, every muscle in his body groaning in protest. Everything that had happened in the past five days was wearing on him, especially Ab Bradley's death. His murder could have been prevented if he'd been able to convince the chief that Angie needed security. Reed hadn't tried hard enough, and it ate at his gut.

He tucked the pillow next to the arm of the couch and kicked off his shoes. He didn't plan to undress. Not when Taylor was around. Her attention on him earlier had about brought him to his knees. She'd taken her time looking him over, her beautiful eyes warming, clear desire there. That was the other reason he'd jumped at moving her to his place, giving him time to cool his jets. Tomorrow, they'd hopefully find her a safe house and he'd only have to see her on a need-to basis.

He pulled his legs up onto the cushion and laid his head back on the pillow, his eyes heavy and burning from lack of sleep.

As he stared at the ceiling, he wondered if Taylor was asleep yet, or was she too, thinking about him. If only she wasn't a victim in a case. He wouldn't hesitate to get close to her. Hell, he couldn't even remember the last time he'd kissed a woman, let alone had a sexual relationship. Taylor was his type. Warm, sexy and smart, though she was struggling right now with this newfound gift. He supposed that would bother most people. Having such frightening dreams and seeing dead people. Yeah, that would send any normal person into a tizzy. Maybe it wouldn't be a bad idea to get her someone qualified in the field to talk to. Perhaps it'd make it easier for her, and that's all Reed wanted. For her to feel able to deal with it without losing control.

His eyes grew heavy. He took in a breath and closed his lids, only to have her image floating around him, in those skimpy pajama shorts and skintight tank top molded to her breasts. His breathing became labored. *Damn it all to hell.* This was the last thing he needed.

Angry, he tore the pillow from under his hand and covered his face with it. Maybe if he suffocated himself, Taylor wouldn't be in his thoughts any longer. With his luck, he'd die, and she'd still be running around in his head in the teeny-tiny shorts—temping him all the way to hell and back.

Chapter Sixteen

Taylor woke and stretched her body, glancing around the room. Not one personal object anywhere. Not even a family picture. Did Reed have a strained relationship with the one sister he spoke of? Did she have any children?

Did he? Why hadn't she asked him?

None lived with him here, but did he have an ex somewhere whom he'd had a child with?

She rose and stepped into the bathroom, the mirror directly in front causing her to do a double take. The dark, puffy circles under her eyes were immense, and the whites around her irises were bloodshot. That's what crying did—made you look horrendous. She needed to curb that right now. Her lip was almost healed, along with her scalp, and her bruising just days away from being gone. She should look better, not worse, and it wasn't even because of her attack, but the man she now stayed with.

Up to this point, Taylor had never allowed anyone to make her feel *less than* like Reed. Time to pack that away. He wasn't worth it. No man was.

She found a towel and turned on the shower. She then went to get her cap and toiletries. In the white-tiled stall, she allowed the warmth of the water to wash over her, relieving the tension in her muscles. Today was a new day, and she was going to find someone to talk to about what she was experiencing. A person maybe having the same visions of people who'd passed over.

Fifteen minutes later, she dragged her laptop over to the bed and opened the search engine. She needed to find someone local. One headline drew her attention. His name was Dean Ambrose. He lived here in town. She clicked on his blog and read some of his entries, intrigued by his encounters, not to mention the fact that he wasn't bad on the eyes. Now, if she could get him to contact her. She wrote a comment on his latest entry, hoping he'd e-mail her, and they could talk in person. That would be her best-case scenario. Or they could speak on the phone if them meeting wasn't an option. Taylor didn't care. She just wanted to connect with someone who could make her understand what was happening to her.

She closed her laptop and glanced around again. What was she going to do now? She hadn't heard anyone moving around in the other room, which meant Reed was still asleep. Going in to make coffee would no doubt wake him, and she wasn't ready to deal with that yet. What Reed would she get today? The sweet Reed, or the one who wanted to snap her head off? That bothered her since she had no idea what she'd done to make him change so drastically, but she didn't like the Reed from yesterday.

Her phone on the nightstand chirped. She reached over to grab it, noting a strange number. With shaky fingers, she clicked on the text, shocked that all it said was *Hi*.

Taylor looked at the number again. Could one of her friends have gotten a new phone plan and was forced to change their number?

She texted back. *Who is this?*

All she got back was a laughing and winking emoji.

She swallowed hard, then wanted to block the number but thought she'd better show it to Reed first. If it was who she assumed it was, it might be important to see who the number belonged to first. Then she could block it.

If it was her attacker, now he knew her e-mail, phone number and where she lived. Did he also know where Reed hung his hat? Was she even safe here? Would she ever be safe again? How could she possibly live a normal life with this guy on the loose?

A knock at the door made her jump. Reed stuck his head in, a mug of steaming coffee in his hand. "I thought you could use this."

Taylor rose and went to retrieve it, handing him her phone. "I received a strange text just a few moments ago. They wouldn't say who they were."

He looked at the message. "I'll call the precinct and see if I can't get the number traced. I'll be right back."

Ten minutes later, he ambled back into the room, placing her phone onto the nightstand. "Looks like it came from a burner phone. There's no way to trace it."

"Now what? This guy has access to everything about me. How did he get it?"

"That's surprisingly easy. A background check is as simple as paying a fee and voila, everything including any parking tickets you may have gotten in the past five years. This guy knows his way around computers, so they might not even be a record of him doing this. Go ahead and block the number. You don't need terrorizing you."

Taylor grasped her phone and did as instructed,

blowing out a frustrated breath.

"Now what?"

"I need to go to the hospital to talk to the man who tried to help Angie. He's awake. An officer will be here to stay with you. I shouldn't be gone long. I'll bring some groceries back, though, I do have some eggs in the fridge if you want to make some."

"I'm fine." Taylor wasn't hungry. She hadn't been for a while.

"You need to eat since you didn't have dinner last night."

"You go ahead and do what you need to do. I'll be fine." Taylor knew Reed was trying to be thoughtful, yet she could still feel that distancing he'd put in place yesterday. She would give anything to know why.

A knock on the front door made Reed turn. "I'll be back soon."

She sucked in a ragged breath, disappointed with his dismissiveness, something that was hard for her to take.

She sat on the edge of the bed and took a sip of her coffee, wrinkling up her nose at the taste. What she wouldn't give for a Frappe from The Perk right about now. She'd love to be there, sitting with her friends, watching people come and go, laughing and enjoying the day.

Taylor had always been a people watcher, loved to think about what their lives were like, which was probably why she was so good at her ad job. Speaking of, she had one, and a campaign to work on. She flipped open her laptop again, finding six new e-mails in the corner. She was almost afraid to look.

Bravely, she clicked into her inbox, surprised to find one from Dean Ambrose. She opened it, happy to see he'd given her his cell phone number and asked her to call him.

She punched in his number and waited. On the third ring a husky voice answered.

"Hello, Mr. Ambrose?"

"Yes. Who is this?"

"I'm Taylor McClain. I left you the message on your blog."

"I'm so glad you called. Your comment intrigued me. You said that you've had a near-death experience."

"I believe so. I was dead for a while before they were able to bring me back. Unfortunately, I've had some disturbing dreams since, ones that seem to be connected to the man who tried to kill me."

"You don't say? Anything else you care to share?"

"I've seen people that are there one minute, then gone the next. Yesterday, I talked to someone who had died the night before. I don't think he knew he was dead."

"And you'd never had this kind of thing happen before your attack?"

"No. Not ever. What about you? I read some of your posts. How did you handle learning that you'd come back with a new gift?"

"To be perfectly honest, not well. It took me finding someone with a similar experience to help me deal with it all. I mean, at first, I thought I was going crazy. It took weeks to figure out that it was all real and that I was given this special gift for a reason—to help these newly departed people find a way to cross over."

Taylor didn't know what to say to that. Was that her mission as well? She had no idea.

"I know this is all a lot to take in. Maybe you and I

should meet and talk about this in person."

She'd love to if that were possible. But Reed wouldn't like her leaving his apartment alone, especially after the events from last night.

"Can I get back to you on that? Right now, it would be difficult."

"Of course. Call any time."

Taylor clicked End Call and took a deep breath. This man was using his experience to help these troubled souls. Could she do the same?

She looked at the five other e-mails she'd received, one with the header, Hi again. Was it the same as from her text? She clicked on it, finding the same laughing and winking emoji. Yet, this time the IP address was different. God. He was tormenting her from every angle. She wanted to block the e-mail address but knew Reed would be angry about that. Likely, they'd just find the same problem as last time, but she couldn't take the chance.

She snapped her computer shut, determined not to look at it again, or at least until Reed returned. Now, she'd try to do something else and hope it'd distract her enough to put the attacker out of her mind, at least for a few hours.

****

Reed stepped into the hospital room, notebook in hand, hoping Brock Evans could give him some much-needed information.

As he neared the bed, the man turned, his face pale, his blue-green eyes cloudy. He was damned lucky to be alive considering the way he looked. "Mr. Evans, I'm Detective Brentwood. I came by to ask you some questions. Do you think you're up for that?"

He nodded.

"Okay, great. Can you remember what happened to you?"

"Yes," he said in a weak voice.

Reed smiled. "What can you recall of the events?"

"I was coming out of James Tavern and saw a man in a black hoodie standing over another guy lying on the ground. A woman was huddled next to a wall, screaming to stop. I ran to help and was attacked. The guy stabbed me before I even knew what was happening. Before I went down, I could hear sirens blaring in the distance. I guess the guy did too and took off running. I remember trying to reach the woman, but I went down. Next thing I knew, I was being hauled away on a gurney."

"Did you see the man who attacked you?"

"Not his face, no. It was dark and he wore that hoodie. I did see a ring on his left hand. It was silver with a symbol of something in the middle of the band. Something weird. A design I'd never seen before."

"Do you think you could draw it for me?"

The man frowned. "I'm not sure. Maybe."

Reed flipped his notebook to the next page and handed him the pad and pen.

Mr. Evans flinched as he tried to draw something on the paper.

"We could do this another time if you aren't ready." Reed hated that he was putting the victim through this so early.

He shook his head, continuing to draw something on the pad, and handed it back to him.

Reed looked at it, noting that it appeared Nordic to him, but he'd check with an expert first. "Was it on the hand that held the knife?" Reed asked.

He nodded again. "Yeah."

So that meant the man was left-handed, which would help narrow the search field again. Also, he was married. That would eliminate Silva for sure. Reed had done a quick background check on him and he was single.

"Anything else you can remember, Mr. Evans. No matter how small?"

"Actually, now that you mention it, he smelled funny."

Reed frowned. "Funny, how?"

"I'm not quite sure. Like alcohol but not in a drinking kind of way. More medical."

"Like rubbing alcohol?"

"Yeah, something like that. Oh, also he picked something up before running. Some kind of container."

That fit with what Taylor had dreamed. The cooler with ice. He'd planned to take a part of Angie with him. *Sick fuck.* Reed would love to know what this nut was doing with these body parts.

"Thank you for your time, Mr. Evans. You'll have a protective detail until the guy is caught.

"I appreciate that."

Reed left the room, studying the picture the man had drawn. It looked like a Viking ship with some type of symbol above it. He'd run it through their database and see what came up. That meant a stop at the precinct before getting some much-needed groceries.

He hoped Taylor was behaving herself. This morning, she seemed different, though in a way her distancing herself was good for him. He couldn't allow himself to get more attached to her. It would be so easy to fall head over heels, allow things to get complicated and then him lose everything he'd worked for. She was just that appealing. Yet, he had to fight tooth and nail to keep that from happening.

Twenty minutes later, he was at his desk checking on the ring. He found the exact picture of the band. Viking. What did it symbolize to the man wearing it? If he knew, maybe Reed would be about to narrow in on the killer. He printed out the picture of the ring and went to get the copy, running into the chief on the way.

"I wanted to say how sorry I was having not listened to you about that woman. I was wrong, and now we have another murder."

"It could have happened to anyone of us, Chief. I just need to get this guy before he has a chance to do it again."

"Do you have any new leads?"

"I do and I'm working on them right now."

"Then I won't keep you." Chief patted him on the shoulder and walked away.

Reed grabbed the photo, intent on doing just that. He was going to catch this killer, and he was going to do it before this butcher murdered again.

Chapter Seventeen

Taylor glanced around Reed's apartment, pleased at how a little tender love and care could change the place. The officer who'd come to watch her was stationed outside the front door, and she had needed something to keep her busy. She'd spent the last three hours straightening up and was happy with the outcome. Cleaning had always been her go-to when things got rough, and everything had started to pile up on her.

She tucked the towel in the arm over the oven door and smiled. Rattling of the front door had her racing from the kitchen to see if Reed was returning.

He'd stepped through the door, grocery bags in his arms. When his gaze moved around the room, they widened. Was he angry she'd tidied up his place? It was hard to tell.

He closed the door with his elbow. "You've been busy." He headed for the kitchen.

Taylor followed. Was he mad? Would he tell her if he was?

While he was putting away a half gallon of milk in the refrigerator, he turned back and said, "Thank you. This is the best this place has ever looked."

Taylor smiled. "I clean when I get anxious."

"I could tell that by how squeaky clean your place is."

"Did that man who you went to see tell you anything

about the guy who attacked them? Did he see his face?" She wasn't sure Reed would tell her, but she wanted to ask anyway.

"No. He didn't see his face. He was wearing that hoodie."

She inhaled a breath. "So, he couldn't tell you anything?" Would they ever be able to catch this guy?"

"Not entirely true. I learned that he wore a ring on his left-hand finger, which suggests he's married. The band itself is also unique. I have some feelers out on that right now. I should hear something soon."

Taylor hadn't seen a ring, but that didn't mean anything. Not really. She was shown what she was shown. No more, no less. But the fact that Reed was telling her things again made her feel better.

When he finished unloading the bags, he placed the empty ones under the sink and turned to her. "I bought some of that coffee you had at your place since I liked it so much better than the stuff I have. Also, I ordered us Chinese food. It should be here in about," he glanced at his phone, "five minutes."

He opened an upper cabinet and brought plates to the table, then retrieved silverware and glasses. "I got iced tea. Would you like some?"

"I'd love some." Yes, this was the Reed she liked. The Reed that made her feel safe, the one she could easily fall in love with.

He quickly poured two glasses and was putting the container away when the doorbell rang. "I'll get it." He quickly left the kitchen, then returned with a large paper bag and placed it on the table. One by one, he pulled out white containers with metal handles and Chinese symbols on the side.

She looked at seven different boxes. "Are we feeding an army?"

"I wasn't sure what you liked so I got a little bit of everything."

"Just a heads-up, you can never go wrong with a good vegetable fried rice."

"Thanks for the tip. I believe we have some of that here." He winked at her.

Yep. This was the Reed that made her stomach flip, and warmed places in her body no other man ever had. But she wouldn't admit that to him since he didn't feel the same.

She sat down and opened a box, happy to see it was the one filled with her favorite. *What were the odds?* She poured some onto her plate and then handed it to him. "You didn't happen to get any Crab Rangoon, did you?"

He smiled again, one that showed off a mouthful of straight, gleamingly white teeth. "I believe it's here somewhere."

Taylor swallowed hard. There wasn't a thing about Reed Brentwood that didn't stir something wild inside her. Too bad she couldn't act on it.

They opened box after box, both going for the unopened one at the same time, fingers making contact. Their eyes met and held for a moment, Reed the first to look away.

"Sorry." Taylor drew her hand back.

"Look, Taylor, I don't want you to feel like you are walking on eggshells around me. I'm sorry for snapping at you yesterday. I was angry with what had happened with Ab Bradley, and I took it out on you. I want us to be friends."

Taylor wanted more than that, but she knew he

didn't, so she'd settle for his friendship. It was much better than them avoiding one another, which was difficult in close quarters. They had to be together, so they might as well do it on good terms.

"I'd like that, too."

"Okay, great. Now, eat. You need to keep up your strength." He dug into his own food, and Taylor did the same.

She hadn't realized how hungry she was after working all morning. Once she'd had her fill, she sat back and studied his features, in awe of his strong jawline, peppered in dark stubble. His nose was perfectly proportionate to his face and his eyes were bluer than the bluest sky.

Taylor gulped, fighting the urge to reach across the table to touch him. *Get your mind on something else.* "You said the ring this guy wore was unique. Can you tell me how?"

"I can do one better. I can show you. He reached into his jacket pocket and pulled out a piece of paper, unfolded it, then handed it to Taylor.

She studied the band, wondering what the significance was to the killer. Did it mean anything to him? Or did it mean something to the woman he married?

"Wedding rings are given to one another, right? Are you thinking this band was given to the killer by his wife and means something to her? Camila picked out her husband's band. He didn't even get to see it before their wedding. I'm not sure if everyone does that, though."

"I hadn't even given any thought to that. You could be right, and this band is more a symbol to his wife than to him."

Jerri Drennen

"Yes, it looks like a Viking ship. But what is that symbol over the craft?"

Reed frowned. "I wasn't sure what that was either. That's why I called in an expert on Nordic folklore to find out."

"Speaking of doing some research... I contacted someone who has had similar experiences after a near death. We spoke on the phone for a few moments this morning. He'd like to speak in person if that's possible. Do you think I could meet with him?"

"Of course you can, Taylor. I want you to do what you need to, to understand this new gift of yours. If meeting with this person helps, then I'm all for it. I could drop you off and wait outside. Whatever makes you comfortable."

Taylor nodded. "I would appreciate that. Would tomorrow be okay if we could arrange it?"

"That's fine. We're in a waiting game on certain things right now anyway. I need to call Travis and see if he's expanded his profile. We can do that over the phone. Go ahead and set it up if you can."

"Great." Taylor rose. "I'll go do that now and come back and help you clean up.

He shook his head. "You've done enough cleaning for one day. I can take care of this."

Things were finally looking up. She was going to get help dealing with this new gift of hers, and she now had an understanding with Reed, one she hoped to build on. Her interest in him went way beyond what he expected, but she planned to change that, one way or another. Reed Brentwood had better look out because she was coming to get him, and he was going to enjoy every minute of it.

****

Reed was happy to see Taylor more at ease with him. He gathered the boxes from the table and placed them in the refrigerator. Even after picking up some things at the store, it still looked bare.

Hell, he was hardly home and had always eaten out. There had never been a need to have much food around until now. He just had to remember this was only temporary. Taylor would be leaving once they found her a safe house. Then she'd be someone else's responsibility.

Why didn't that soothe his mind like it should? Because he didn't trust anyone else to keep her safe, not for one day or for even an hour, now that he thought about it. Every minute he'd been away, he'd worried the whole time. Pictured the hooded killer getting his hands on her again.

He took in a labored breath, pushed the thought aside and finished clearing the table, rinsing and placing the dishes in the dishwasher, then turning it on. Another thing that had always been empty, hardly ever used. Did he live here, or was it simply a place to store his shit? Pretty much the latter. Maybe it was time for him to have a life beyond work, beyond going from one investigation to the next, not having anything else. What kind of life was that really? Why had he allowed himself to get so wrapped up in his job that nothing else mattered? With that, he could picture his life in retirement, alone, unhappy, wondering why he'd let this obsession with work rule the day.

It was stupid. But things would have to change after he caught this killer. Other lives were at risk. That was more important right now. He'd think about making some life decisions after this case was resolved.

His phone ringing brought him back to the present. He walked to the table and picked it up, not recognizing the number.

He answered the phone. "Brentwood."

"Yeah, Detective," a man said in a voice barely above a whisper.

"Yeah, who is this?"

"This is Vince Silva. I need to talk to you right away."

"Well, talk." Reed was irritated with the man. He didn't have the courtesy to give him the information he'd asked for days ago.

"I can't right now. It's about that woman who was attacked at the gym. I think I might know who did it."

"Why can't you tell me over the phone?"

The phone then went dead. *What the hell.* Reed pressed redial. Silva was going to tell him, and he was going to do it now.

He let the phone ring seven times before giving up. Now he was going to have to go talk to him tomorrow. But how, when he'd promised to take Taylor to see that person? This was going to screw up everything.

Taylor returned to the kitchen, worry lines etched on her forehead, a frown on her lips.

"What's wrong?"

"He couldn't meet me tomorrow. He has to fly out tonight for a family emergency. He won't be back until Thursday."

"I know you're disappointed by that. I'm sorry. Unfortunately, I just got a call and I'm going to have to leave you again early in the morning. I need to go meet with someone. "

"Okay. Well, I guess everything worked out for the

best, then."

Reed could see how disappointed Taylor was and he wished he could help, but he had no way of understanding what she was dealing with. Seeing the newly departed seemed like a made-for-TV movie to him, yet he believed her. No way could she have known Ab had died in that hospital, and her then seeing him. He had no doubt that she'd talked to him since her dreams had been spot-on every time. Her life-after-death experience had given her a new insight, and Reed was going to use that ability, if at all possible, to catch this killer.

Chapter Eighteen

Taylor watched as Reed left his apartment, disappointed that she couldn't go along. She was starting to feel like a trapped animal in a cage she couldn't escape. Up until this happened, she was on the move every waking moment of every day for the last year. Now, she had too much time on her hands to think, especially about the man who attacked her.

Why had he singled her out? Why pick women who had the same characteristics? What was it about her hair color and the shape of her face that made her a target?

Taylor should do some research on serial killers and what made them tick. It wasn't like she had anything else to do right now. Reed's apartment was spotless, and TV had never been her thing. Maybe she could get inside this guy's head further than she had in her dreams. It might help Reed find him.

That in mind, she walked to his room to retrieve her laptop and brought it back to the living room. What kind of search would work? Serial Killing 101?

Yeah, no.

Maybe reading some of the news stories about the killings themselves would be the best place to start. She typed in women murdered in the city, and Sylvia Moore and Jamie Denton's names came up, along with an older woman who died almost a year ago. She'd cross her off since Travis seemed to think this killing spree had just started.

Taylor read over some of the articles, finding no real detail that she herself hadn't already known. Just that the women had been murdered, no suspects in custody. The more articles she read, the more frustrated she became. She clearly had more knowledge about these women's killings than the reporters did.

She snapped the laptop shut, shoving it to the side. What next? This isolation was for the birds. Was this what people felt like in prison? Even they got yard time. Where was hers? Taylor was going to lose her mind if she had to spend another day like this.

She rose from the sofa and paced the floor. Maybe she could do some floor exercises or find a good workout video on YouTube. First, she'd change into something suitable, if she'd even brought anything like that with her. When she was packing, she'd been so distracted that she'd just stuffed as much into her bag as she could. Hopefully, there were gym clothes there somewhere.

She retraced her steps back to Reed's room, still wondering why the man had no personal items anywhere. Did his life completely revolve around his job? Why else would he not have anything that represented any social interaction beyond that? It seemed sad to Taylor. Did he even have any friends?

She reached down and tossed her bag on the bed, unzipped the top, rifling through the content. She came across her favorite set, a light-peach sports bra and matching leggings. She stripped down to her underwear to change into the gear. Now to find a workout that she could do for an optimal effect.

Taylor was happy that Reed's kitchen island was high enough that she could place her computer there and have room to work out. After finding one that looked high impact, she clicked on the instructions and followed along, the pace and movements easy to get the hang of. Forty minutes later, she was in cooldown mode when the door came open and Reed stepped inside. His eyes darkened as he looked her up, then down. Did he like what he saw? She hoped so.

She wiped sweat from her brow, waiting for him to say something. Nothing came. He continued to stare at her, the muscles in his jaw clenching.

Something was running around in his head. Taylor would love to know what it was.

"Did you talk to the person you planned to?" Her question made him look away.

He shook his head. "I couldn't find him."

"Are you concerned by that?"

He shrugged. "I'm not sure."

She shifted from one foot to the other. "Have you talked to Travis yet today?"

"I did, but he wants to meet in person to talk about everything. I suggested we have lunch. You up for that?"

"Are you serious?"

He nodded.

"I could kiss you right now."

His eyes widened.

"Don't worry. I'm not really going to kiss you, Reed. I'm just excited about getting out for a while. I was going stir crazy here."

"I'm sorry about that. I wish it didn't have to be this way, Taylor, but it's only until we catch this guy. I'm hoping that Travis can help facilitate that with his advanced profile."

Taylor nodded. "I hope so too. I'd like to get my life

back. Camila will be home in another five days, and I promised to help her get settled into her new home. I don't plan to miss that, since I had to bow out of her wedding. You have no idea how hard that was for me. We've been best friends forever. The last year of my life was wrapped up in planning that wedding I didn't get to witness. I'm not doing that when she returns from her honeymoon. I'm warning you about that right now."

His mouth opened then shut again. He clearly didn't know what to say to her. What could he say?

"I'll go get cleaned up and then we can go." Best to get out while the going was good. Taylor was afraid he'd refuse her demand. He could try. It wouldn't work. If need be, he could help paint while she was at Camila's.

The thought made her smile. And if truth be told, she wanted the two to meet. Maybe Camila could tell her how unrealistic it would be to think Taylor could have a relationship with Reed, even though that was what she wanted. Him, on the other hand, probably not. But she still wanted Camila to tell her what she thought. Then again, was it even worth trying with a man who didn't seem to have any social life? Her best friend might have a better perspective on that and say yea or nay to him.

Taylor turned on the shower while tucking her hair under the cap. In another few days, her scalp would be healed enough that she would no longer need to use it.

Inside the stall, she turned her back to the spray, her body erupting into a series of goose bumps when she started to think about Reed again. What was it about this man that made her want him so badly, especially since he didn't seem to feel the same way?

She pushed the troubling thoughts away and rushed to finish her shower.

Back in the bedroom, she found a pair of black slacks and a white, button-down top and dressed. Sitting on the edge of the bed, she pulled on a pair of boots and grabbed a sweater and left the bedroom. Reed was in the kitchen, drinking a glass of water. He looked troubled by something.

"Is everything okay?" She started toward him.

"Are you ready to go?"

Deflecting her question. Why?

"Sure." Taylor followed him from the room and out of the apartment, taking in a deep, cleansing breath. She was going to be happy and put her concerns behind her. She was out, and that's all that mattered now.

****

Reed drove into the parking area of the Highland restaurant and cut the engine. Being with Taylor was becoming increasingly difficult. When he'd returned from Silva's apartment and walked into his, Taylor had been in a skimpy exercise bra and skintight leggings, and it had left him hot and bothered. How much more could a man take? He wasn't a saint, for God's sake. He had a libido and frankly, it was torturing him just to be next to her now.

He opened his car door, the fresh air helping to clear away her exotic scent. When he came around, she was waiting for him. He was thankful that Travis would be here to get his mind back on the job.

Inside, he led Taylor to the archway of the main dining area, stopping to look around. His friend was tucked in the corner, away from everyone else. Reed had to smile since he knew a few choice things about the man, one being that he was an introvert. He didn't like crowds and always found a secluded area to be alone. He

144

was a lot like Reed in that respect.

Travis waved them over. "I was wondering if you changed your mind."

"That was my fault," Taylor jumped in. "I couldn't decide what to wear."

"It's quite all right. It gave me time to go over my notes again."

She took a seat next to Travis and Reed sat across from them both.

A young man stepped over to their table. "Can I get you two a drink?"

Reed looked to Taylor. "Coffee would be great."

"Make that two."

When the waiter left, Reed focused on Travis. "So, what did you come up with since we last talked?"

"You have four men who are interesting, to say the least. One, an Everett Sides, surprisingly was a cop in Oregon in the late nineties."

Reed's eyes popped open. "How old is he?"

"In his early sixties, and under any other circumstance, I'd instantly eliminate him, but with the law enforcement background, I can't."

"He'd know the ins and outs of how not to get caught. But his age must be considered."

Travis nodded. "Yeah, but let's keep him on the list for now."

"Okay, then who are the other three?"

"Did you get a chance to meet with Herman Litman?"

That was the one man who was never home when Reed came by his house. "I tried. He was never around, and I couldn't get him on the phone."

"Weird guy. He works at Public Water and Power. I

145

couldn't find much on him other than he's in his early forties, never married, and rents the house he lives in. You'd think a man his age would own something, right? He doesn't even have a car. How does a guy making seventy-five thousand not own anything? Yes, he has a 401K, but there isn't a large sum of money there. Where does he spend it all?"

Good question. Even if he wasn't the killer, was there something going on with this man that'd need to be checked out? It might be a good idea to recon his home. See if he was hiding something.

"How about the third guy," Reed asked.

There is a personal trainer that could fit the profile yet couldn't find much on him either. Work history is scanty at best."

"Is it Vince Salva?"

"Yes."

"I met with him, and he could be. The guy was evasive for sure, and a prick. So, who is number four, then?

"Randall Morris works at a funeral home."

"But he wasn't a suspect. He was the person who found Taylor."

Travis rubbed at his jaw, glancing back at the papers he had in front of him. "I guess I didn't see that in your notes."

"It might have been a small notation. That means we're down to just three men, then?"

The waiter returned to take their order, giving Reed a chance to glance over at Taylor. Why did she have to be so darn pretty? And sexy. When he looked at her, he saw her all sweaty, in that revealing workout gear, and all he could envision was having hot sex with her.

He looked away and took a long drink of his water. The thought of going back to his apartment with her and being alone without touching her would be a feat in itself.

He blew out a long, agonizing breath and shifted into his seat. "You okay, Brentwood?" Travis asked, shaking him out of his uncomfortable thoughts.

"Just tired." It wasn't a lie. He'd barely slept in days.

Travis studied him intently, then a smile curled up his lips. Why, Reed could only imagine. Was Reed's attraction to Taylor that obvious? Would he take him aside and give him a good talking-to, or let it go? If he chose to speak up, Reed hoped it wouldn't be in front of her. He didn't want her to know he was drawn to her because she didn't need that. Taylor had enough on her plate. Reed hardly wanted to be the one to add to it.

Chapter Nineteen

Taylor stepped out of the bathroom and went to lie in Reed's bed, sniffing the pillow and sighing. Even with them being clean, the soft material smelled like him, a plus, though his mattress was hard and lumpy.

Hours ago, they'd returned to his apartment without saying more than a few words to one another. Something was bothering him, and she could tell he didn't want to talk about it.

Was he distracted by Travis's assessments? She had no idea, but she'd give anything to know what was running through that head of his. In the few days they'd been together, she'd concluded that he was quiet and somewhat brooding, the total opposite of her. They were clearly not a good match, but then again, opposites did attract, and she was drawn like a moth to a flame to Reed.

Too bad he only noticed her when she was in skimpy clothing. Hmmm. Maybe that's what she needed to do. Dress in revealing workout gear and see where that went.

She shook her head. That was stupid. Either the man wanted her, or he didn't. She couldn't force it. No matter how badly she'd like to.

When she heard Reed talking to someone, her ears perked up. Was he on the phone? She didn't hear any knock, so he had to be.

She rose and walked to the door, pressing her ear to the surface to hear better. He raised his voice, and she quickly opened the door to find out what was happening, remembering too late that she was dressed in her pajamas.

He looked at her, his eyes widening. He then said "okay" and ended his call.

"Is everything all right?" she asked.

He turned back to her and shook his head. "That person I went to see this morning still hasn't surfaced. That worries me. I should have gone to see him right after he called."

"Does this have to do with my case?"

He nodded.

"Are you sure he's missing?"

"Well, he didn't show up at his job today, and his employer said that's unusual for him since he gets paid in cash and he likes money."

Taylor chewed on her bottom lip. "Do you think he might be dead?"

"That, I don't know. As we speak, there's a uniformed officer going to the apartment complex manager where he lives to get the key to his unit. They'll let me know if anything is found."

"You want me to put on a pot of coffee?"

"No. I'm too wired to drink caffeine. But if you'd like some, go ahead."

Taylor got the feeling he just wished she'd go back to his room, and that was the last thing she wanted. "Can I ask you a question?"

"Of course."

"Do I make you uncomfortable?"

His eyes widened for a moment. But would he answer her?

"Uncomfortable, how?"

"The last few days you've seemed different. Like I did something wrong. Yes, you've told me you'd like us to be friends, but you don't give me that vibe. I feel as if I make you nervous when I enter a room."

He stared at her for a moment, then appeared as if he was about to say something but instead shook his head. "You don't make me uncomfortable, Taylor. I'm just used to being alone. Please don't think that I don't want you here."

Why didn't she believe him? Sure, he looked sincere, yet there was something in his eyes that spoke otherwise. Something about her bothered him, and she was determined to find out what.

"Okay, if you say so."

"I do. Now, stop worrying, and go get some sleep. I'll wake you if I need to leave for any reason."

What could she say to that? He wanted her to go to bed, and unfortunately, she was in no place to say no. She'd head to his room and try to sleep, though she wasn't sure how easy it would be.

Back on the bed, she closed her eyes, and an image started to form in the back of them. *A dark-haired man lying down with his back to her, big and brawny, not moving. She watched closely, waiting for the rise and fall of his chest, but nothing came. Was he dead?*

She moved around his body until she could see him from the front. The man's eyes were wide open, like he was awake, yet the deep, bleeding cut across his throat spoke a different story. Instantly, his face jogged a memory. He'd been at the gym the day she was attacked. He was the man spotting another. The instructor.

Taylor jerked awake, holding in a scream desperate to come out. Who was the man? Was he the one Reed had been trying to find? Would the police officer sent to his apartment find him there? Why was she being shown all these horrible things?

She sat up in bed. Should she tell Reed about the dream, or keep it to herself? She didn't know what to do.

For now, she would leave him alone. He was probably asleep anyway, and she didn't want to wake him. He didn't get much rest and needed it more than she did.

She leaned over to the nightstand and grabbed her laptop. Until her eyes got weary, she'd work on her ad due in a few days. She had put it off long enough.

She quickly found her file for the account and went to work. Minute after minute ticked by, finishing up the last detail at 2 in the morning. She was happy with her work and would send it to the office when she got a chance.

As she was getting ready to close her computer, an email popped up; it was from Dean Ambrose. Excited, she opened the email and quickly read it, overjoyed that he returned home early and wanted to meet with her that afternoon. Taylor couldn't be more thrilled with the prospect. She quickly wrote him back, agreeing to meet him at his home at one. Now, she was never going to be able to sleep, looking forward to what he'd say about her experience and possibly being able to help her cope with this gift of hers. Even the strongest of individuals would have a hard time seeing dead people and dreaming of such horrors. Maybe he could give her some tips on coping with them. Clearly, there was a reason she'd come back with this ability, and she wanted to do the right thing with it. With his help, perhaps she could.

****

Reed woke and turned, a crick in the neck making him flinch. *Dammit all to hell.* That's what he got for sleeping on the couch. His bed might not be as comfortable as Taylor's guest bedroom's mattress. Much better than the alternative. The too-short sofa where his feet hung over the arm. He sat up, trying to rub the pain from his muscles, to no avail. He was going to need a painkiller and a hot shower to ease the tension.

His phone ringing had him reaching across the coffee table to grab it to answer. "Brentwood."

"Detective, this is officer Anderson, we didn't find anything at Vincent Silva's apartment. I just thought I'd better call and let you know."

"Thanks, Officer Anderson."

Reed ended the call and tossed the phone down. Where the hell was Silva? Was he hiding? Why call him and ask to talk and then just disappear. It didn't make any sense. Unless something or someone caused him to vanish. That was Reed's biggest fear since he could have possibly prevented it. Silva worked at the gym where Taylor was attacked. Maybe he'd overheard something or saw something he shouldn't have. The only positive was that Vince's body hadn't been found. Maybe he was alive and lying low.

The door to his room opened and Taylor walked out, already dressed, looking not at all rested. "I'd ask if you slept well but it's pretty clear you didn't."

"I had another dream that woke me."

Reed straightened. After the last three nightmares, he'd learned to take them seriously.

"What happened?"

"I saw a man from my gym. I think he was one of the personal trainers. I saw him lying on the ground with his back to me. I walked around and found that his throat had been slashed.

"Shit." The word came out before Reed could contain it. Silva was dead.

"Could you see anything that could tell us where the man was?"

"Not really. At least, I don't think so."

"Come sit down. I'll try the technique like we did with that tavern."

She came and sat in the chair adjacent, her floral scent instantly bombarding him. God, she smelled good. *Get your mind back on track, Brentwood.* This was too important to get sidetracked.

"Concentrate on what you first saw."

"A man was lying on the ground. Right away, I noticed how muscular he was."

"What was he wearing. Do you remember?"

"A T-shirt. Dark blue or maybe black. Shorts. Black too, I think."

"Was he wearing shoes?"

"White tennis shoes. I saw them as I was walking around him. They looked expensive. Those trendy kind that cost a day's pay."

"Was there anything around the shoes? Cement? Wood flooring? Grass?"

She chewed on her bottom lip. "Yes. It was concrete."

"So, let's keep going. You said you were walking around him. Were you looking down? Or around the room?"

"I was looking at him, then as I stepped around his body, I looked up for a moment."

"Okay. What did you see?"

"I saw a window. It was narrow and I could hardly see through it because of all the grime."

"And you were looking up and not across from the window?"

She frowned. "Yes, but what does that mean?"

"To me it suggests it's a basement."

"Oh, you're right. I can see the concrete walls now. You are so good at pulling things out of me. How did you learn such a skill?"

Reed sighed. Was it a skill? He didn't know. It was just something he'd always been able to do.

"Okay, you saw the concrete walls. Anything else that you can see?"

"There's an old calendar hanging from a peg."

He nodded. "What's on the calendar? Anything you can point to."

"It's like one of those old pinup pictures. You know of those girls for the forties, maybe."

"Can you see a year on it?"

"Hum...nineteen... Sorry, I can't read the rest."

He smiled at her. "No. You did great. Let me write all this down. I'll be right back."

He quickly found his notebook and jotted down everything she'd told him, then stepped back into the living room, finding Taylor checking her phone.

"Trouble?" he asked her.

"No. the guy who has a similar gift to mine came back early and wanted to know if we could meet today. Could we possibly do that?"

"Of course. Did he specify a time?"

"We'd talked about afternoon, but something came up for him. He's asking if ten would work instead."

"Ten, it is. I'll go take a shower and get ready. Don't

answer the door. Anyone knocks, come get me."

"Okay."

He went to his room, noticing that she'd tidied up and made the bed, something he rarely did. Another thing the two were completely opposite about. Even if he could date Taylor, they were so unalike, he didn't see how it could work out. Yes, opposites attracted, but did any really stay together? He doubted it.

In the bathroom, Reed stripped down and stepped into the shower, turning on the water. The cool spray shocked his senses and caused goose bumps to erupt over his body. He quickly adjusted the temp, turning his back to the water, hoping it'd ease the strain in his neck muscles. As he was soaping up, he heard his phone ring. *Shit.* It could be something about Silva. A knock on the bathroom door had him feeling exposed. "Yeah." He leaned his head out of the shower.

"Travis is on the phone. He wants to talk to you."

"Tell him I'll call him right back."

"All right."

Reed rushed to finish his shower, then toweled off and walked to the bedroom and dressed. He wasn't sure what Travis needed to talk to him about, but it had to be something important. Maybe it'd be what they needed to break the case and bring a killer to justice.

Chapter Twenty

Taylor was taken aback at how handsome Dean Ambrose was. With his wavy blond hair, green eyes, and a friendly smile, which seemed to ease any tension she had at meeting him. "Come sit down, Taylor, and you can tell me everything you've experienced since your near-death event."

She took a seat across from him, folding her hands in her lap, contemplating how much to reveal. Case-wise, she really shouldn't tell him anything. Reed wouldn't like it. But she could tell him the basics.

"I've had several dreams coinciding with real events that have happened since my attack. It's almost as if I'm connected to the man who hurt me in some way, in his head somehow, watching him."

His eyes narrowed, and he frowned. "I can't say that I've come across anyone with similar gifts. Maybe it's a way for you to help them find this guy. You said you've seen people who have passed on. Tell me a little about that."

"The first time I saw something strange was at a bar. A man in clothes that didn't seem to fit the decade was sitting in a booth, no drink in front of him. He saw me watching him. I turned away for a moment and he disappeared. I also felt a chill pass through me moments before I turned back."

"That's a typical sighting. When it's safe to do so,

you need to go back to that bar and see if you can help him cross over. There's a reason he's stuck there, and maybe you can help to find out what that is. The longer it takes for a soul to cross over, the angrier that soul gets. Bad things can happen then."

"How do I help him?"

"Ask him why he's there. See if he answers."

It gave Taylor the willies to even think about going back to where she saw the man. "Maybe you could help me?"

"If that would make you feel better about it, I'd love to help. You and I could aid each other. This gift we both have can be hard to deal with sometimes. We could be one another's buffer when it becomes overwhelming." He reached out and clasped her hand, a gesture that was kind yet didn't spark a single reaction like Reed's touch had. That spoke volumes. She and Reed had a strange connection that had nothing to do with her gift. It was chemical and powerful. Too bad he didn't seem to feel the same.

"Is it possible for this to go away after a while? Could it be temporary?" In a way, Taylor hoped it was since it made her doubt her sanity.

"I've never heard of it coming, then going, but I haven't met all that many people with this gift. Is that what you want? For it to go away?"

She shrugged. "I don't know. I just want my life back. Is that too much to ask?"

"Not at all, Taylor. You'll find, after a short period of adjustment, that this will become the new normal."

Taylor didn't see how, but these were early days. Maybe she would adjust to it in time.

"You also said that you'd met a man at the hospital

who had just died, right?"

"I did. He was looking for the woman he was with when he passed. According to the detective that's protecting me, she was there at the hospital in the Psych ward. I hope he's not haunting her. She's going through enough with what happened."

"We need to do something with him. Just in case he is. We don't want another ghost on our hands. Can we persuade your detective friend to take us to the hospital and see if you and I can't help this person cross over?"

Dean's idea was a good one. If they could help Ab and protect Angie from being haunted, it would be a win-win.

"I'll go out and talk to Reed. I'll be back in a few minutes."

She knew Reed would agree. Yet, since he'd spoken to Travis, his mind had been distracted. She'd love to know what they talked about. Reed was such an inward person, the total opposite of her. Maybe he could help tone her down some and she could bring him out more. Perhaps that's why certain people attracted opposites, to change things each couldn't without help.

She found him leaning against his car, soaking up the beautiful day. His eyes were closed, his face up, enjoying the sun. Reed probably didn't get to spend much time just being. No one today did. They were all in too much of a hurry. Maybe this new gift of hers was to teach her to appreciate her life more since it was almost cut short by the monster in her head.

As she stepped down off the covered porch and walked toward him, his eyes opened, his lips curling into a smile—one that literally took her breath away. There was something about this man that made her want to be his, and his alone. Forever.

"Would you be able to take Dean and me to the hospital to see if we can't help Ab cross over? If he hasn't been able to yet. I'm afraid if he's still there, he might be trying to find Angie, and that right now could cause her to shatter."

"I can do that. After, we're going to need to try and find that basement."

"Deal." She headed in to get Dean. With any luck, they could cross Ab over and find where that basement was, and the body of that poor man, who could have likely been another victim of this hooded killer.

****

Once at the hospital, Reed had no idea how Mr. Ambrose and Taylor planned to help a dead man cross over, but he wanted to be there to keep her safe. For the half an hour she'd been at the man's house, he'd allowed himself some much-needed time to soak up the sun and cool breeze of the perfect spring day. A rarity for him.

Hell, since on Taylor's detail, this was the most time he'd taken off from working practically twenty-four/seven the past two years. And he'd survived. Maybe his job wasn't everything it'd been cracked up to being in his life. Perhaps it was time to reevaluate what was important to him.

"When I saw Ab, he was in the basement." Taylor's words drew Reed out of his meandering thoughts.

Reed opened the door and allowed both her and Dean to step into the hospital and then followed. "Let's take the stairs. Just in case he's hovering between floors," she said.

As they were walking down, Reed noticed the way Ambrose watched Taylor, and it sent his stomach into throat. The man was interested in her. Then again, who wouldn't be? She was beautiful and smart and sexy and…*shit*. When did she become so important to *him*?

They'd reached the landing and Taylor stopped. Dean turned to Reed. "He's here."

Reed couldn't see a damned thing. He hated that this was something Ambrose and Taylor had in common. This would only strengthen their bond. Leaving him left out. Alone again. Naturally. Damned song, and its relevance in his life.

"Do you know you're dead?" Dean asked.

"No. Angie will be all right. We'll make sure of that." Taylor looked near tears.

"Have you seen a bright light? If you do, go toward it. That's where you'll find peace," Dean said, placing his hand on Taylor's shoulder.

Pure, unadulterated rage filled Reed. He wanted to shove the man away from her but knew that wouldn't be wise. Not when they were trying to help this man cross over. Besides, Taylor wasn't his. She could choose who she wanted to be with. Not that he'd even given her an option. He'd always tried to steer clear of her. Maybe that needed to change now. If he wanted her, he had to tell her, or she might find Dean Ambrose more to her liking.

Taylor turned to him and smiled. "He's gone."

"Are you sure?" Reed looked at Dean, who nodded.

"So, that's that?" Reed had no idea how all this worked. Before Taylor and her dreams, he'd never believed in ghosts and these kinds of premonitions, but she made him a believer. And frankly, he was in awe of her gift.

"That's how this works, yes." Dean smiled at

Taylor. "This is why we need to band together. We could help so many souls."

Reed squinted and studied the man closely. He was going to need to run a background check on him. See what came up. Yes, it could be his jealousy working overtime or it might not be. He was still going to do the check. Just to be on the safe side.

"Can we go now? I have a meeting to get to," Reed asked, wanting to get Taylor away from Ambrose. If he was some kind of charlatan, intent on using Taylor's gift, it was best she didn't spend any more time with him.

Taylor frowned.

Okay, his tone had been overly sharp, but he did need to meet with Travis. Something strange had come up with the man who had discovered Taylor behind the gym, and the two of them needed to go over his story. Could he have lied? Made up the whole thing to throw them off track? That, Reed needed to find out.

They left the hospital and returned Ambrose to his home. He hoped that would be the last time Taylor would see him. Perhaps Reed was being cautious, or maybe jealous. Either way, he hoped he'd seen the last of Dean Ambrose.

The drive to his complex was done in silence.

"What's going on with you?" Taylor asked once they were behind closed doors of his apartment.

"What do you mean?"

She placed her hands on her hips, her beautiful eyes narrowing. "You've been acting strange since we were in the stairwell at the hospital. Do you think we were lying about talking to Ab?"

"No." What should he tell her? The truth? Was he really ready for that? Was she? Reed didn't know.

"I don't trust that Ambrose character. He seems like an opportunist to me."

"How so? What do you think he's after? That doesn't make any sense to me, Reed."

He swallowed, knowing this whole thing with Taylor was going off the rails. Reed had no right to tell her something that he couldn't prove. Until he ran the background check, he should just keep his mouth shut.

"Well?" She now looked downright annoyed with him.

A knock on the door saved him from answering. "That's got to be Travis."

He walked to the door and peeked out the peephole. It was Travis and he looked about as grim as Reed felt at that moment.

Chapter Twenty-One

Taylor sat at the table, still trying to figure out why Reed had such an aversion to Dean. Everything had changed in that stairwell, and she'd give anything to know why.

Travis shoved some papers at Reed. "Read through his statement and tell me what you see?"

She had no idea what was going on, but she was determined to find out.

"He's got some inconsistencies in his story. He said he left at around seven, but another person at the gym said he'd gone some twenty minutes earlier. Why would he lie about the timing unless he didn't check his watch or phone at the time and was just guessing.

"That's why we need to interview him again. Also, I have a few questions I want to ask this Litman character. I read over the officer's interview with him from yesterday morning at his place of work, and he noted that Litman seemed nervous. Why would he be so jittery if he was innocent? I think we need to call them both in for an interview and see if either man cracks."

"I agree." Reed pulled his cell phone out of his jacket pocket.

Taylor sat back, numb to that fact that one of those men could be her attacker. That this person would have killed her if not for someone stopping them. Her head started to spin out of control, her heart thumping crazily in her chest.

Reed glanced at her as he waited for an answer. "Are you okay?"

Was she? Not really. Her heart was working overtime, and she could barely breathe. It was like in the hospital, after her first nightmare. Somehow, she needed to calm down. The nurse had given her something then. Here, she was on her own. *Breathe in, breathe out. Now repeat until you can breathe normally again.*

"Taylor." Him calling her name brought her attention back to him.

She gulped, then said, "I'm okay."

Both he and Travis looked uncertain if that were true.

"I'm all right."

"He's not answering. I'll try the other," Reed said, looking frustrated. He punched in the number, his eyes connecting with hers, their color deepening. What was that all about? Did he suddenly find her attractive? Why? What had changed in the past six hours? Dean Ambrose perhaps. Was he jealous? Was that why he'd gotten all pissy about the guy?

Inwardly, Taylor would jump for joy if that were the case. But how could she find out? Maybe she could try to kiss him and see what happened. With that thought in mind, she couldn't wait for Travis to leave.

"He's not answering either. Why have a cell phone if you aren't carrying it around?"

"Or maybe they just don't want to talk to you," Travis interjected, frowning. "In the morning, you and I need to stop by their places and talk to them together. With that plan, let's meet for breakfast first. Early. Before they have a chance to leave for work. I'm in no mood to have to visit a funeral home."

Taylor cringed at the idea. She'd only been to one in her life and that was when her grandmother had died. She was six at the time, and the memory still haunted her, was why she didn't go to her grandfather's funeral. Death had been so foreign to her up until she'd been attacked, now it was bombarding her every waking moment.

"Good night, Taylor." Travis's words drew her out of the troubled thought.

"Good night."

Reed walked him to the door and then secured the lock and chain. He turned back to her, looking uncomfortable now. What the hell was it with this man? He ran hot and cold, like a faucet. Taylor had no clue how to deal with that. Most of the men she'd dated were like her. Happy and self-assured. Not moody and distant like Reed Brentwood. How could the two ever have a relationship since they were so different?

Truth be told, they probably couldn't, but she still wanted to know what it felt like to kiss him. Just once.

"So, I thought we could watch a movie or something. Maybe order a pizza?" Taylor suggested.

"If that's what you want. First, I need to work up a series of questions for those men tomorrow. It should take me fifteen minutes. You'll find a number for the nearest pizza place on my fridge. Go ahead and order what you'd like. I can eat anything."

Taylor nodded, then went to the kitchen and quickly ordered a large deluxe and then returned to find Reed sitting on the couch, a notebook in his hand, scribbling something down.

"It's ordered. They said about forty-five minutes."

He looked up from his work. "Great. Now, find us a movie to watch."

Taylor found the remote and brought up his apps. She clicked into one of his paid subscriptions and scrolled through the options, thinking a romantic movie might set the mood for the kiss she planned to get one way or the other. Whether he wanted it or not.

She smiled to herself. If he knew what she was planning, how would he react? Would he run for the hills? Or revel in the idea? She sure as hell wished she knew.

What if she kissed him and it led to something more? Her skin heated and she shifted on the sofa.

Then again, what if she kissed him and he pushed her away? That would be devastating to her ego. Was she willing to take that chance? Her head was reeling with all these lingering doubts when the doorbell rang. She was about to get up when Reed stopped her.

"I'll get it." He rose and walked to the entrance, peeking out the peephole, then opening the door. He quickly paid the deliveryman, then secured the locks and brought the pizza box over and set it on the coffee table. "You want some tea?"

She nodded, watching him leave, then return with two glasses. She had to admire his swagger, the way he commanded a room. He was a manly man, unlike most of the guys she dated. Anyone in PR advertising dressed to the tees, had manicured nails and two-hundred-dollar haircuts. Reed was so different, so much more. Too bad she didn't know how to appeal to him.

She pressed start on the movie, and they ate in silence. Either she'd kiss him, or she'd chicken out. Only time would tell which she'd choose.

****

Reed could tell something was on Taylor's mind, but he wasn't sure if she'd confess to what, if he asked.

He swallowed a large drink of tea, the collar of his shirt becoming increasingly uncomfortable. Just sitting next to her, watching a love story, was causing him to think impure thoughts. But then, hadn't he decided that all work and no play was ruining his life? What was he getting out of it besides being alone and unhappy?

An overwhelming need to touch her vibrated from every cell in his body yet he didn't act on it. It'd been so long since he'd been with a woman, he'd forgotten how. How pathetic was that? *Pretty damned.*

He cleared his throat and shifted on the sofa, causing her to turn toward him, their eyes connecting—and holding. Reed couldn't look away even if he wanted to.

Then, without provocation, she slid closer, and her mouth came down to brush his, so softly that he barely felt the kiss. She drew back and stared at him.

Now what? Would she kiss him again? Should he kiss her? *Shit.*

Reed sucked in a breath, unsure of what to do. He was so bad at this. But he did want to kiss her again, this time with a little more passion, more feeling put into it.

He was going to take the chance and see what happened. All she could do was reject his advance.

He leaned in and pressed his lips to hers, gently at first, waiting to find out if she would reject him. She didn't pull away, instead she met his pressure with her own, igniting a fire inside him. He cupped her neck and drew her in closer, his mouth melding to hers, causing an explosive reaction in his groan. Heat flooded his entire body, and all he could think of was getting closer, wanting the pressure of her body next to his.

He released her neck, and with both hands on her shoulders, he pulled her next to him, his tongue working on the seam of her mouth until she opened, and he explored the sweetness inside. Everything about Taylor filled him with a sense of wonder, in ways he'd never imagined. All he could do was revel in the experience as he worked his hands down her back, her skin heating at his touch. A positive in his mind. Maybe she did want him as much as he wanted her.

That driving him, he eased her back onto the sofa, and half covered her body with his, hoping that his hardness didn't shock her.

His mouth left hers and he worked his way down her neck, intoxicated by the subtle floral scent floating in the air around her. She moaned in his ear, and that alone drove him to a frantic state. He wanted them skin to skin, exploring each other, building a fire only they could put out.

A buzzing sound—one he tried to ignore—finally caused him to look up at her, confused. She appeared oblivious to the incessant noise. Instead, she tried to kiss him again, but Reed looked over to see that his phone was lit up. *Dammit all to hell and back.* He had to answer it.

He reached for his phone and clicked answer. "Brentwood," he said, barely recognizing his voice. "I'll be there in twenty minutes."

He ended the call and glanced back at Taylor, whose eyes had narrowed. She was angry he'd answered the phone. She didn't understand that his job was twenty-four/seven. Not a nine-to-five like hers.

"You'll have to come with me. We have another

murder."

She inhaled. "But I didn't dream it? Why didn't I see this one?"

"Actually, you did. They found Vince Silva in the basement of one of the men Travis profiled. Come on. We need to go."

On the way out the door, Reed grabbed his keys off the stand, and he allowed Taylor out before locking the door behind them. If what Reed was thinking was true, they now had Jamie and Sylvia's killer dead to rights. Why else would he murder Vince Silva? Vince had found out something about Litman and confronted him, then was killed. Clear-cut to Reed. Now, he just needed a confession to wrap it all up. Hopefully, in the next few hours, he could get one.

On the drive to the scene, Reed's mind went haywire. He and Taylor had almost done something that could have cost him everything. Why had he allowed his body to supersede his brain? Now, he was going to have to tell her that he'd made a mistake and that it couldn't happen again. He'd let Dean Ambrose's interest in her overshadow his integrity. Reed knew better but had allowed his loneliness to get in the way.

Up ahead, he spotted the flashing lights and parked next to a patrol car, an officer standing out front. He'd leave Taylor with him, then go to the scene. He knew she'd seen Silva's body in her dream, but to witness death in real life would be too much for her to take. She didn't need that.

Chapter Twenty-Two

Reed placed Taylor in the hands of a young officer and walked away. She was still reeling from their passionate encounter—angry he'd chosen to answer his phone instead of finishing what he'd started. Clearly, Reed loved his job and it'd be hard competing with that no matter how much she wanted to.

She held in a sob, frustrated that she was allowing her emotions to get the better of her again. Before her attack, nothing or no one managed to faze her resolve. Now, everything sent her into a spiral—yet another reason to despise her assailant.

She sat back in the seat of the squad car and stared at the house in front of her. Things could be worse. She could be the victim inside. That alone brought her back to reality.

She dug her phone out of her purse and noticed a text from her best friend. She'd be back in a few days, and she had to be allowed to welcome her. She didn't care what Reed said. Not when he didn't seem to care how she felt.

—*We need to talk*— the text said.

Why would Camila have to talk to her on her honeymoon? It didn't make any sense.

—*What's up*— she typed back.

Her friend immediately started replying. Something was wrong. But what?

She waited for her friend's text to pop up, her heart rate accelerating.

—I found text messages on Gavin's phone from his assistant telling him she was pregnant with his child. I'm leaving him. I'm on the plane now, getting ready to depart. I'm going to need you when I get there.—

Taylor's jaw dropped. Never in her wildest dreams would she have imagined this scenario. What was she going to do? She had her own set of problems, and yet she knew her friend was hurting and needed her.

No way could she go back to her condo. She glanced at the house again. Or could she? Have they made an arrest? Seemly so. Why would she still need protection?

Taylor sent a text back telling her she'd pick her up from the airport and let her know what time she'd be arriving.

—Plane lands at six in the morning. Smilie face emoji.—

She looked at the time on her phone. She had nine hours before she'd need to be there. In the meantime, she'd have to figure out how to get away from Reed and back to her condo to get her car that had been delivered to her home two days ago.

While logistics ran through her mind, Reed stepped out the front door of the house and started her way. It was showtime. Somehow, she had to get her stuff and get back to the condo without anything else happening.

How could her and Camila's life be imploding at the same time? Only two weeks ago, she was on her way to getting a big promotion at her agency and Camila was marrying the man of her dreams. Now, both were in a bad place. Something neither would have ever believed in the month leading up to the wedding.

Reed stopped to talk to the officer who stood in front of the patrol car where she sat and spoke to him in a hushed tone. Taylor only able to catch a few words.

He then came and opened the back door and stuck his head in. "Officer Shields is going to take you back to my apartment. I need to go down and interrogate the suspect. I have no idea how long it'll take, but Shields will see that you are taken care of until I return. All right?"

"And you're sure this is the guy who attacked me and murdered those other women?"

"Vince wanted to tell me something before he was killed, and he was found in this guy's basement. So, I'd say, yes."

Taylor couldn't have asked for a better chance to be able to get to the airport, though she'd need to somehow distract the officer so she could slip out. She'd just need to be ready.

"Fine," she said in a tone that wasn't quite hospitable. She didn't want to draw any suspicion. Reed was good at reading her, and it was too important for her to get to Camila when she arrived.

He nodded then closed the door right as the officer jumped into the driver's seat.

Taylor sat back and ran through her mind how she'd get him into the apartment, then get out without him knowing. Once she returned to her condo, she'd pack an overnight bag, and she and Camila could travel to her grandfather's cabin. On the way, they'd pick up things they'd need to spend a few days there, giving them both time to decide what was next. The two could deal with anything as long as they were together.

Back at Reed's, Taylor placed her purse on the table

next to the door, then went to retrieve her laptop, the one thing she'd need to take since staying in contact with work was essential. They'd given her a few weeks to recuperate, but she still needed to answer any emails or problems that arose.

She tucked the machine into her bag and placed it next to her purse. Now all she had to do was wait for the officer to use the restroom, then she planned to bolt. Once she was free, she'd call for an Uber. Then, she knew she only had a few extra minutes to pack a few clothes, get in her car and head to the airport. No one would think to look there, and she could spend her time thinking about why she'd allowed herself to get so caught up in Reed Brentwood when he could turn on and off on a dime.

****

Reed sat across from Herman Litman, the sweat rolling down the man's face, him fidgeting in his seat. Who wouldn't be, since Vince Silva's body was found in his basement and there was a steep price to pay for murder?

"Tell me what happened, Herman?"

"I don't know. I had nothing to do with the guy's murder. I didn't even know he was in my basement."

"Right. What you're saying is that someone put him there?"

"That's exactly what I'm saying. I did know Vince from the gym, but I had no beef with him. What is my motive for wanting him dead?"

"Well, perhaps he was getting ready to tell us that you attacked the women in the parking lot."

Herman shook his head. "No. I didn't touch that woman. Someone's trying to frame me."

Reed planned to play along with his ruse for a while. "Who would do that?"

"I don't know. Isn't that your job?"

If Reed wasn't a seasoned detective, Litman's comment would have made him laugh. "My job, Herman, is to find out why you killed Silva since he was found dead in *your* basement."

The man's eyes widened. "I've been set up. Why can't you see that?"

"Why would anyone want to dump a body in your home to make you look guilty? Who'd have access to your place to be able to put Silva in the basement without being seen?"

"I don't know, but that's what happened. You must believe me. I had no reason to kill the man. None."

Litman was a great actor. If the guy hadn't been caught dead to rights, Reed might have questioned if he could be telling the truth. But how could that be?

"Look, Detective, I have a fruit cellar in the back of my house that leads to my basement. The door lock has been broken for a few weeks. I haven't had time to fix it. Whoever killed Silva could have brought him in through that entrance even if I was home at the time. Would you at least investigate that?"

"Why? It doesn't make any sense."

"Don't think I don't know how strange this all sounds. I wouldn't believe me either if I didn't know I was innocent. I just need for you to keep an open mind about someone wanting to throw the scent off them by setting me up for the murder."

Reed stared intently at the man. The more he talked, the more Reed started to question his guilt.

"I had a friend running a background on you and

there were a lot of odd things that came up."

"Like what?"

"Like why don't you own anything? You have no car and you rent the place where you live. What do you do with all your money?"

"I don't have a car because I don't have a license to drive one, and home ownership is not all it's cracked up to be. I work forty-plus hours a week and I don't have time to fix a damned lock on a cellar door, let alone a roof or a furnace. I'm not good at that shit. Not everyone wants to have those kinds of responsibilities."

"Then why don't you have more money in the bank or in a 401k?"

"Because I help my mother, who's in a nursing home. Do you have any idea how much it costs to keep someone in one of those places?"

Reed was instantly taken aback by what Litman was telling him. Now, all the bizarreness wasn't so bizarre anymore. It was all explained. Maybe Reed was going to have to go look at that cellar door after all. He could be telling the truth.

And if that was the case, a killer was still on the loose. Thank God an officer was with Taylor.

"All right, Litman. I'm going to look into your claims. Hang tight."

He scowled but no way was Reed letting him go until he found out for sure he was innocent or not.

As he left the interrogation room, he ran into Travis.

"Well?" the man asked. "What do you think?"

"I'm going to follow through on this cellar door thing. See if he's telling the truth. If that's the case, I need to know why someone would frame him for Silva's death."

"That's self-explanatory to me. Throw us off to kill Taylor, or another woman he's been watching."

A sick feeling formed in the pit of Reed's stomach. Had the murderer done this so that he could get to Taylor? That seemed a likely scenario, one that sent a cold chill through in body.

He needed to get to her.

"I have to leave. I'll get back as soon as I can." Once Reed was in his car and backing up, his phone went off. He quickly answered. "Brentwood."

"Sir, we have a problem."

"What kind of problem?"

"While I was in the restroom, Ms. McClain left. I tried to find her, but she was gone."

"Jesus Christ," Reed cursed. "Have someone go to her condo and see if she's there. I'm heading that way now. We need to find her."

Reed stomped down on the gas. He knew something Taylor didn't. That they probably had the wrong man in custody. No doubt so they'd be looking the other way while this fiend nabbed her.

In minutes, he was pulling up to Taylor's condo and jumping out as an officer stood pounding at her front door. He saw Reed and shook his head. That's when Reed noticed that her car was gone.

Shit.

She'd been here and then left in her vehicle. She could be anywhere right now.

He took out his phone and found her number, allowing it to ring seven times with no answer. She was angry with him. He knew that. That's why she refused to pick up or answer any text messages. But Taylor had no idea that she was in grave danger and wouldn't until it was too late.

Chapter Twenty-Three

Taylor's heart soared when she saw her best friend coming through customs. She was so happy to see her, Camila's swollen, red eyes instantly hindered that joy.

She raced toward her, wrapping her arms around her back, tightening in a death grip. They were lucky they had each other right now.

When Camila pulled away, her eyes were filled with unshed tears.

"Let's get your bags and get out of here. I thought we could go out to Grandpa's cabin and spend a few days. We'll just turn off our phones and spend time trying to figure out our next steps. What do you think?"

"I think that sounds perfect. We can stock up in Reynolds for essentials. Ten bottles of wine and maybe some food."

Taylor smiled. This was the Camila she knew and loved. She'd get through this betrayal and come out on the other side stronger and wiser. Taylor would, too.

Thirty minutes later they were headed out of town. "Tell me what has been happening with this investigation?" Camila reached over to squeeze Taylor's right shoulder.

"They have a suspect in custody right now. Detective Brentwood is interrogating him as we speak."

"That's good, right? Why do you sound disappointed?"

Was Taylor ready to get into this with her friend right now? Maybe she should wait until they were a bottle of wine in first.

"Let's talk about you." Changing the subject was best. "Why were you in Gavin's phone?"

"He was in the shower and his phone rang. I answered and the line went dead. I glanced at the name. It was one of the women he works with at Martin and Lawrence. That's when I found the texts. I didn't say anything. Instead, I waited for him to fall asleep, then wrote a dear Gavin letter and slipped out. I was lucky to get a flight back home right away. I found ten missed calls from him and five texts pleading with me to forgive him. I didn't respond. I should have seen this, Taylor. I'd been so busy with the wedding stuff that I was blind to his always being gone."

Taylor glanced at her friend. "Don't you dare blame yourself, Cam. This was all on him."

"I know but it hurts to know after all these years he'd do something like this. Why marry me? It doesn't make any sense."

"Piss on him," Taylor said matter-of-factly.

"Yes. Right. Piss on him, and the mother who birthed him. I never did care for the woman. At least now I won't have to spend Christmas with her."

Taylor cracked up laughing. This was what she loved about Camila. She had a sense of humor, and she wasn't afraid to use it, even in a bad situation.

Once they'd stopped at a local grocer and picked up supplies, it took them twenty minutes to get to the cabin in the middle of the woods. Only a handful of people knew the property belonged to Taylor. Seven years ago, she'd inherited the twenty-five acres, cabin with two outer buildings, all fenced to keep people out. One side facing the enormous lake. The man who had gifted her the place sidestepped her mother, why, Taylor still didn't understand, since her mom refused to talk about it. She didn't seem at all bothered that she hadn't inherited the land. Maybe someday Taylor would ask.

They exited the vehicle, and Taylor grabbed the bags from the back. Camila reached the porch and turned to look at her. "Keys above the doorframe. When we get everything unloaded, I'll go to the shed and start the generator."

An hour in, both had settled onto the sofa with a glass of wine in their hands. Taylor knew questions were going to come, and she was formulating in her mind what to tell her friend about Reed.

"So, I want to know why you aren't happy about this arrest."

"No, I'm relieved they caught this guy. Don't get me wrong. It's just that there's more happening than I was ready to tell you in text messages. Weird experiences that I've been having."

"Such as?"

"I need to give you some context first. I learned a few days ago that I was dead for a few minutes at the hospital, but they brought me back. I've been seeing strange things since. People who have passed over."

Camila raised a hand. "Wait. What?"

"In the famous words of *Sixth Sense*, I see dead people."

Camila's mouth gaped.

"I know it's hard to take in. Imagine what it's like for me to be seeing them. I thought I was going crazy, and it didn't help that I was barely sleeping because of the horrible nightmares.

"What kind of nightmares?"

"Dreams about past and present murders, and one that was about to happen. Seems I now have some type of connection to my attacker. I can see what he's doing."

"Oh my God, Taylor. That's the most frightening thing I've ever heard. Have you talked to anyone about it?"

She nodded. "I've talked to Reed and to a man with a similar experience, though he only sees the dead people."

"Who's Reed?"

"Detective Brentwood."

Camila studied her intently. "You are on a first-name basis with the man?"

Taylor looked down, not sure whether to tell her about what had happened between them.

"Are you two…well, you know?"

"No, we haven't had sex. We shared a kiss. I don't think he likes me as much as I like him."

"Well, probably because he could lose his job if anyone found out about this inappropriate relationship, Taylor. Police officers can't fraternize with their victims. It's against policy."

Taylor had wondered about that. She just didn't know for sure. But this could explain why Reed had held back. She wouldn't want to jeopardize his career. That wouldn't bode well for a strong relationship.

"Like I said, it was just a kiss."

"But you wanted more?"

"I did, but now I see how stupid that was. I could have destroyed his life. I'd never want to do that."

Camila smiled. "You really care for him, don't

you?"

Yes, she did. Now that she accepted that, she needed to realize what he'd been dealing with. Perhaps he had found her appealing, and would have liked to act on it, but couldn't because of his job. That alone made her care for him even more.

"So, now that we've established that both of our life's are fucked-up, what do we do next?" Camila asked, then took a long draw on her wine.

"We drink until we forget our problems." Taylor took her own long drink. Things were indeed fucked-up, but at least they had each other, and that would help them both get through this.

****

Reed clenched his fists and took a ragged breath. They'd put a BOLO out on Taylor's car, but nothing had come up yet. She'd been gone for hours now, and he was starting to wonder if her attacker hadn't gotten to her.

He'd tried calling her twenty-plus times with no answer. He'd even left several voicemail messages to no avail. She was missing, and he had no idea where to look for her.

His only option was to go back to her home, search for clues and hope that gave him a lead.

He pulled into her driveway and was quickly ushered into her place. Officers were there waiting in case she returned.

Reed went straight to work, rifling through her cabinet drawers, hoping to find something—anything that'd give him a lead to follow.

An hour in, he slammed a drawer, frustrated that he'd found nothing. Maybe there was something in her bedroom.

He stalked to the room and switched on the light, finding one of her drawers open. Reed stepped over and looked inside. Lacy underwear was folded neatly in rows, about four or five pairs missing. Had she taken them to his place, or had she returned to pack a bag? He reached in and ran his finger over a peach-colored, silky pair, angry she'd gotten so far under his skin. His blood burned for her, and he didn't know what to do about that.

He shook the thought and walked to her closet, opening the door. Everything inside smelled like her. *Shit. Stop it.*

On an upper shelf was a lockbox, a key in the hole. He took it down and placed it on her bed and unlocked it. On top was an envelope that read deed. Was that to her condo? He unfolded the top and pulled the paperwork out, a description of property stunning him. It was in Whelps County. A parcel of land with a cabin next to a lake. Maybe this was the place in the picture in the guestroom, and Taylor was given it by her grandfather. Could she have gone there to get away? This was the only lead he had. He might as well take it. He quickly wrote down the address and walked to the guest room to look at the picture to get a better idea of how to get access to the cabin, then left. It'd take him over an hour to get there. He just prayed that her attacker wasn't two steps ahead of him.

On the drive, he tried to call her again, getting her voicemail every time. "Dammit, woman. Why aren't you answering?"

His mind was running one scenario after another, all ending with Taylor dead. If she would have just stayed put. She likely thought she was safe since they had a suspect in custody. Too bad he probably wasn't the right one.

He took the road his navigation told him to, then things got harder. The place was out in the middle of a forest, and where to turn was iffy at best. The dark made it even more difficult.

Ahead, he saw a road, one that didn't look like it'd been used much. That was probably his turnoff. He cut right and drove down the narrow path, his heart ready to jump out of his chest. She had to be here, and she had to be alive. Otherwise, Reed didn't think he'd ever forgive himself for leaving her with the officer.

Chapter Twenty-Four

Taylor was working on her third glass of wine and feeling its effects.

Camila tried to stifle a yawn. "I think I'm going to crash. It has been a very long day for me."

"All right. See you in the morning. I'm just going to finish this." She lifted her glass. "Then I'll be right behind you."

"Goodnight."

"Night." Taylor gave her friend a smile.

When Camila was gone, the room closed in on Taylor. Maybe she shouldn't have had so much to drink, especially in her state of mind. Altering her brain chemistry with her newfound visions probably wasn't the smartest thing to do.

A creak of a floorboard had her looking to see why Camila had returned. No one was there. *What the hell?* Now, she was hearing things.

Her life was never going to be the same. She had these gifts that she didn't want, but there was no way to get rid of them.

She placed the wine glass down, thinking it best not to finish it. Alcohol just amplified her problems.

She rose. Time to go to bed and hope tomorrow would be better for both her and her best friend. Camila was sleeping in the guest room. Taylor was taking her grandfather's old room. She hadn't been there since she'd arrived and wasn't sure how she'd react.

At the door, she sucked in a breath, then stepped inside and flipped on the light. Everything in the room was old, out-of-date, but reminded her of the man himself. She closed her eyes and inhaled, imagining him. She'd never really gotten to know her grandfather, but what she did know about him, she liked. He was a hardworking man. Wanted little for possessions and had integrity. Kind of like Reed.

The thought made her open her eyes, widening them when a glowing form materialized. Her grandfather stood before her, a grimace on his face. "You need to get your friend and hide," he said in a stern voice. "He's coming."

"Who's coming?"

"Hurry. You're running out of time. There's a secret door in the study, behind the portrait of your grandmother. Go now or it'll be too late."

Then he disappeared.

Taylor raced to get Camila and shook her awake. "Come on. We have to hide. The man who attacked me is outside."

"What?"

"We have no time for this. We must go now." She tugged at her best friend's arm.

The two ran from the room and Taylor led them to the study, where she placed her hand next to the portrait and a panel slid back. Inside was a small room. "Get in."

Once inside, she pulled the handle and closed them in, every nerve in her body charged. Somewhere in the house, glass broke, and her ears perked up.

Camila gasped. Taylor placed a hand over her friend's mouth and put a finger to her lips, then waited, every noise making her heart clench a little harder.

This whole thing didn't make sense. The killer was supposed to be in custody. How had he found her? Footsteps close by had her holding her breath and Camila's eyes popping open. *God.* What had she gotten her friend into? This was her mess, not her best friend's. She'd had enough distress with her husband messing around on her. Camila didn't need this horror.

Someone moving around the room brought her back to their dilemma. *Please don't let him find us.*

There was nothing. No movement. No noise for what seemed like an eternity, then she heard footfalls off in the distance. He was leaving the room.

She slowly let out a breath and squeezed Camila's hand, too scared to do anything but listen. Hopefully, he wouldn't return and find their hiding place. Because no way could they survive if he did.

For what seemed like hours, the two stayed in the room, both in tears, holding each other's hands tightly.

If they lived through this, Taylor was never going to take anything for granted. She was going to live her life to the fullest and try to help as many lost souls as she could along the way.

A knock at the front door made Taylor jump. She was too afraid to leave her hiding place. What if the attacker was trying to draw them out? Then both of their lives would be lost. The knocking started again, then a familiar voice called out her name. *Reed.* "It's Reed."

But where was the killer? Was he between her and Reed? What should she do?

She leaned over and whispered for Camila to stay put, then eased open the door and peered out, not seeing anyone. Maybe the guy left when he heard Reed coming.

187

She made her way to the door of the study and peeked out, only a short distance between her and the front door where Reed stood. Could she make it there, unhook the chain and bolt-lock before the attacker could get to her? The hairs on her arms charged. She had to do something. Standing there all day wasn't going to secure her and Camila's safety. That was for sure. She was going to have to chance it and hope her luck held. If not, she and Camila could both die, and it would be her fault for hesitating.

****

Reed knew he was at the right place when he spotted Taylor's car. With his weapon drawn, he'd stalked up the steps to the porch that wrapped around the rustic cabin and went to the door. There were lights on inside, though at this late hour, Taylor could be asleep. He'd knocked, listened for any noise from inside. He didn't hear anything but the sound of crickets, tree frogs, and howling of coyotes off in the distance.

Then he knocked again and called her name and checked the door. It was locked. No way could he get in. *Dammit all to hell.*

"Taylor," he called out louder, thinking she must be asleep and couldn't hear him. Should he go around to the back and see if he could get a glimpse of her through a window?

A scrambling of feet and a chain rattling brought his attention back to the door. When it came open, the frightened look on Taylor's features put him on alert. She pointed inside and Reed aimed his gun and forced Taylor behind him as he moved around the room, searching for whoever had her so upset. Fifteen minutes in, he found blood dripping from the jagged glass of a broken window. Had the intruder gotten it coming in or going out? Reed wished he knew. Then again, he couldn't find anyone inside. Maybe that meant the guy left when he heard him coming up the road. Though, he could be watching them right now, waiting for another opportunity to get to Taylor. And that was never going to happen, not while Reed was alive. He'd come to some conclusions while trying to find her. His feelings for her were strong, and even losing his job wouldn't squelch them.

"Let's find something to cover this window," he said. It was best to stay put until morning. Then they'd head back to the city.

They were about to step out of the bedroom door when Reed heard crying coming from somewhere. "Is someone here with you?"

"Oh, God. Camila." She raced from the room.

Reed quickly followed, shocked when Taylor popped a wall panel open and revealed a beautiful, dark-haired woman, tears amplifying her stunning, crystal-blue eyes.

This must be Taylor's best friend, but why was she here? Hadn't she been on her honeymoon?

Taylor tried to comfort her, and the response touched his heart, made him care even more for Taylor. She was an amazing person, kind, smart, talented, and he wanted her to be his. He knew that now.

"Camila, I want you to meet Detective Brentwood. He's the man working my case. He'll keep us safe."

"Hello." She wiped at her tears.

"I thought you were in Bora Bora." He was still confused about how she'd gotten here. There was only one car out front.

Taylor shook her head, indicating that was a subject not to discuss. He'd have to get the 411 on that later, once they were all out of harm's way.

"You two stay in the living room. Lock the door. I'm going to find something to block that broken window. You hear anything, call out."

Reed left the room, looking in the back for something that he could at least keep the bugs out. He found some Tuck tape and a large piece of cardboard in a small pantry, then quickly got it up in place and taped it. Then he moved a large dresser with an attached mirror over to block out anyone trying to break in again. After that was done, he checked all the other windows, happy to see that the only two not visible had bushy roses growing halfway up the glass. Getting in there would be painful. *Good.* At least it would be a deterrent if her attacker was still outside.

He returned to Taylor and Camila, both sitting on the sofa, looking shell-shocked. Could he blame them? Not really. Thank God Taylor knew where to hide, otherwise they would probably be dead now. That thought alone gave his whole body an artic chill.

"So, why did you leave my apartment today while I was gone?" he asked, not really expecting her to give him an honest answer.

"Camila texted me to meet her at the airport. I needed to go. I'm sorry for causing so much trouble. I thought you had my attacker in custody. What happened?"

"Clearly it wasn't him. He was set up by the man who attacked you."

"I don't understand. How would he know to do that?"

"I believe, and this is just a theory, but the two men we were targeting were both being trained by the dead man in the basement. I think Vince Silva somehow found out something and was killed for what he knew. Setting up Litman was just a way to throw us off the real killer's trail."

"Are you saying you know who the killer is, then?"

"I believe so, but proving it was him might be more difficult. He probably hasn't left anything to incriminate himself. If I had to wager a bet, he's probably been setting Litman up for a while now. He's smart. We just need to be smarter."

They both frowned. Could Reed blame them for being skeptical? "I'll get him, Taylor. You don't have to worry about that. By the way, that's quite the hiding place back there." He pointed toward the study. "Did you used to play in there as a kid?"

Taylor shook her head. "I didn't even know it was there until tonight."

It was Reed's turn to frown. "Then how?"

"My grandfather told me where it was. He came to me right before the attacker broke in. Told me to get Camila and hide."

Reed looked around the room. "Is he still here?"

"No. He told me to hurry, and then he was gone."

This newfound gift of Taylor's had saved her and her best friend's life. Reed wasn't going to think of it in a negative way from now on, even if it cost him her in the process. There was a reason she was given this power of sight, and he needed to understand and let her use this to help others. After all, that's what he'd devoted his life to, finding the killers of innocents so their families could have a little peace.

Chapter Twenty-Five

Taylor covered Camila with a blanket and looked over at Reed. He was watching out the front window, no doubt looking for the man who changed her life in a matter of minutes. She still wasn't sure if she should be thankful for what had happened—being given this gift. But she had it now, so she was going to have to learn to live with it. One thing was for sure, without her grandfather coming to her, telling her to hide, she and Camila would probably be dead. Even with Reed showing up. Time would have been on this killer's side, and she silently thanked her grandfather for that.

She walked over to Reed. "Do you see anything?"

He turned to look at her. "No, but that doesn't mean he's not out there somewhere, waiting, hoping I slip up somehow. I already feel bad that I allowed him to sway me in another direction, giving him a chance to get to you."

"That was hardly your fault. I should have thought things through more thoroughly before meeting Camila at the airport. She could have been killed because of me."

"What happened there? I thought she was in Bora Bora."

Taylor glanced over her shoulder at her friend. She was out cold, but was it Taylor's place to tell someone about her best friend's betrayal?

"Let's just say the honeymoon didn't go well."

Reed flinched. "I'm sorry. Is she going to be okay?"

"With my help, yes. She's a tough cookie. She'll weather this and come back stronger than ever."

His eyes warmed. "Glad to hear it. How about you? You doing okay? I mean, this thing with your grandfather. Are you dealing with that all right?"

"I'm grateful he came. Otherwise, you would have witnessed another crime scene."

"Yeah, that thought plagued me the whole drive here. I called you ten times, and left voicemails. I was so relieved to see you were okay. Promise me you won't do anything like this again until we have the killer behind bars."

Taylor crossed a finger over her chest. "I promise. This was too close a call here. I won't let it happen again. It could have cost my best friend's life."

He reached over and ran his palm up her arm, causing goose bumps to race over her skin. No man's mere touch had ever done that before. There was something about Reed that stirred every part of her, made her want something permanent and forever with him. If only he felt the same.

"Can I ask you a question, Reed?"

"Of course. What do you want to know?"

"If you weren't the detective on my case, would things be different between us?"

His eyes widened, and his jaw clenched tight. Had she hit a nerve or was he shocked by her suggestion?

Seconds ticked by like hours as he stood staring at her, opening his mouth to say something, then closing it again. Was he trying to think of a way to let her down easy? She didn't want that. Taylor needed him to tell her the truth.

"Yes," he finally said. One word. But how did he mean it? Could he be anymore cryptic?

"You are going to need to elaborate on that, Reed."

He took in a labored breath and then let it out. "It's against policy for an officer in law enforcement to have any type of relationship with a victim in one of their cases. I could be fired. That's if they found out, of course. Up until now, my job was everything to me."

She swallowed hard, catching his insinuation. "Until now?"

"You must know how I feel. I've been drawn to you since we first met. I'm fighting hard to keep my head on straight, following protocol, but with you, I just..." He shook his head. "I want to have more than just this job. I want to have someone in my life to come home to. To ground me. To make the hard times easier. You made me see that."

He was saying he wanted someone to help him change his life but was that someone her? She wasn't sure, and this was hardly the time to start something anyway. A killer could be outside, and her best friend was on the couch.

Reed's phone buzzed and he reached into his pocket and glanced at the message.

That alone was something Taylor would have to live with if they got together. His job wasn't nine-to-five. It was twenty-four/seven, and she wasn't sure how she'd deal with that. What if they had important plans and he got called away? How well would she be able to forgive him for that? Why was she suddenly realizing these things? Maybe it was best to take a step back. Look at her life. See how well he'd fit into it first.

She sighed, then went to sit in the chair next to

Camila. It was safe there, where she could think straight. That's what she needed to do before acting on any attraction, no matter how powerful it was for her.

****

Reed watched both women sleeping. Taylor had left him next to the window hours ago, something having changed. He didn't have a clue what, but he felt an instant distancing. A guard she'd put up, and he didn't know why.

Perhaps it was for the best. Could they really have anything together? This whole attraction thing could be imaginary. Some kind of knight-in-shining-armor type of thing, and Taylor finally realized how tarnished his armor was. He was hardly a catch. He barely had anything. An apartment that only looked decent now because she'd cleaned it. Money-wise, he had a little but nothing like she had. What would be her draw to him?

He cleared his throat and looked back out the window. He couldn't wait until morning. He needed to get them out of there and into the safe house they'd finally found her for. If Camila planned to stay too, that'd be okay. At least she'd have her friend there to keep her company. He had to focus on Randall Morris since he was young and strong enough to overtake her, not to mention having lied about discovering Taylor. Travis had texted him some details on the man who ran a funeral home. Supposedly, his mother had died a year prior, and it could have somehow triggered his aggression—his need to murder. But why? And how did he catch the guy with no proof that it was him? At least now he had DNA, but he couldn't compel the funeral director to give his for analysis. So, unless he caught the man in the act, he was grasping at straws.

He did have the boot prints. But to get a subpoena to search his properties, Reed would need probable cause, and he wasn't sure his gut instinct was enough for a judge to give one.

He rubbed at his tired eyes and took a ragged breath. The system failed in a lot of ways. He understood that people had rights, but where were those rights when Sylvia, Jamie, and Ab were killed? The man didn't deserve the same privileges as others did—not when he was a murdering sociopath. The guy deserved to die, and Reed would love to be the one who killed him.

The first rays of light in the distance spoke that dawn was about to break. He was relieved that in another hour or so they'd be on their way to the city, out of harm's way, and Reed could get some much-needed distance from Taylor. Get some perspective. And to do that, he had to be away from her.

He glanced over at her; her face appeared less severe in sleep. Most of the time she looked stressed, and he really couldn't blame her. She'd gone from a woman with a career, no problems, to having a madman chasing her and seeing dead people. Anyone would be losing their shit. Reed sure as hell would be.

Once he was back in town, he was going to find a way to take care of at least one of those things for her. Catch and put away this crazy lunatic, hell-bent on killing her, and any other women who resembled her. Reed could hardly wait to find out what connection there was to that, because it was the key to everything. Perhaps there was a lady from this man's past that he couldn't get over—a woman with the same coloring and features and that's what started his killing spree. If Reed could find that, maybe he could make him slip up and they'd get him.

Reed smiled. *Yep.* That's what he was going to do. He was going to do a thorough background on the guy and use it to catch him.

Chapter Twenty-Six

Taylor glanced around what was to be her new home until they caught her attacker. The place was nice, maybe not as nice as her own condo, but more than what she'd expected. Camila had chosen to stay with her, not even opting to go home first to get different clothes. It's not like they'd be leaving the house anyway, and this way, Camila wouldn't have to confront her husband anytime soon.

The refrigerator and pantry were stocked with everything imaginable, more than enough to get them through for weeks if need be. Hopefully, it wouldn't take that long for Reed to catch this killer and put him away.

They'd driven back in Reed's vehicle with the promise that Taylor's car would be waiting for her at her condo on her return. Driving both to the city was too dangerous if her attacker was watching them. Once back, they'd gone directly to the precinct, then on their way to the safe house, they'd changed cars twice before arriving. No way could anyone had tailed them. She and Camila were safe and would remain that way as long as they stayed put.

An officer would always be present, shifts changing every twelve hours, according to Reed, who had just left. He'd looked relieved when he did. No doubt happy to be leaving her. Then again, she felt the same. With him around, it was hard to think clearly. At least with them apart, maybe Taylor could get some perspective on how she felt. Maybe her infatuation was simply a victim/protector thing. This time apart would give her a chance to figure it out, perhaps talk to Camila about it all. Her best friend had always been able to see things from a different perspective. Taylor needed that right now.

"So, what should we do?" Camila asked.

"I say we both get cleaned up, put on some comfy clothes, make some fattening food, and find a chick flick to watch. What do you think?"

"As long as a glass of wine is included, I'm all in."

Taylor needed to remember what her friend was going through. She'd loved the man she married and to find out he'd cheated and was expecting a child was the ultimate betrayal.

"Wine, it is. Meet you in the kitchen in twenty minutes?"

"Deal."

They went in opposite directions, both bedrooms having their own bathroom. Taylor quickly found a comfy pair of sweatpants and T-shirt, then went to turn on the shower, refusing to let anything distract her from getting in and out. No more thinking about Reed for the next few hours. Both she and Camila needed some downtime.

After showering, she dried off and jumped into her clothes, then walked to the kitchen. What did she feel like eating? As she was digging through the refrigerator, Camila joined her.

"Pasta is always a good choice."

Taylor looked up at her best friend and nodded. "Let's carb out. Maybe it will make us both forget our problems."

"You want to tell me why that hot detective was in such a hurry to leave?"

Taylor shrugged. "I guess he's just tired of being around me."

"No. That's not it. I watched him look at you on the drive back. He has a thing for you."

"But is he willing to risk his job? I'm not sure."

"He's got a lot to lose, Taylor. You get that, right.?"

"Yeah, I understand. I just have to wrap my head around it. I know it's a huge conflict for him. I just wish things could be different."

Her best friend took her by the shoulders. "You and me both. It's hard to find someone you can trust. Look at my life. I thought it was all set. The husband. The new house. Now, everything's shit."

"You know it wasn't always like that. Gavin loved you. I think he still loves you. Why else would he marry you knowing he had a child on the way with another woman? He made a huge mistake, and he lost you because of it. I bet you a million dollars he'd take the affair back in a heartbeat."

Camila shook her head, her dark, wet hair swinging around her, a strand sticking to her face. "You don't know that. Maybe he just didn't know how to get out of it. You know how hard it is for him to say no to me. Even if he didn't like something."

"I don't believe that, Cam. If he didn't still love you, I doubt he would have gone through with the wedding."

"Can we stop talking about this? I just want to eat carbs and forget he ever existed. Okay?"

Taylor nodded, then pulled her friend in for a tight hug. "Carbs, wine, and maybe a little *Vampire Diaries*.

How does that sound?"

"OMG, yes. How did you know that I needed some Damon and Stefan, the brothers Salvatore, to soothe me right now?

Taylor smiled. "I mean, who doesn't?"

They laughed, then went to work to cook their pasta and finding the right wine to go with it.

****

Reed pulled up the search engine on his computer and typed in Randall Morris's name. Travis had a start on the man's profile, but Reed wanted to go deeper.

Link after link came up, the first being the Morris Funeral Home page. He clicked on it and went to their about us page. It'd been in the family for three generations, Randall being the current director, no wife, no children.

Wait a minute. Why had one of the victims seen a ring? Did that mean it wasn't him? Maybe he'd been mistaken about which finger it'd been on. That was more likely. So why was a man his age single? Was he gay, perhaps? Or maybe he just had a problem with women. *Red flag.*

He read everything, then clicked on another link, bringing up an article written by Randall Morris on Viking mythology.

There was that connection. His heart rate increased. He was getting close to catching this guy. But he had to play this just right. He couldn't rush things until he had all his ducks in a row. It had to be iron-clad because he couldn't let this guy walk away—not after killing four people and assaulting two others. He needed to pay with his own life.

Now that they had the guy. Reed needed the why?

Why would he do something so heinous to these women? And why now?

He had to find out about Randall's life. What might have happened in his world for him to start killing women. It was bizarre, yet something had triggered his murder spree. And why take body parts? What meaning did the ritual hold for him?

Reed did a search for his birth records. He was born January 12th, 1979, to Cynthia Grace Jamison and Theodore William Morris. Their only child. That alone was strange unless his birth was traumatic.

Theodore died when Randall was seven. So, that left his mother with the business to run and a young child to care for. It couldn't have been easy for her. Reed did a search on Amelia, and nothing unusual came up. A death certificate was registered less than a year ago. Okay, that might have been the trigger. The death of his mother. But still, why start killing women and take parts of their bodies? It didn't make any sense.

He shut down the computer's search engine and wrote a few notes in his pad. His next step was to go talk to Randall, see if he wore that ring and go from there.

While waiting for the elevator, another thought occurred to him. Did Morris Know Litman well? Why did Randall choose to set *him* up? He couldn't have known he was a suspect. So, why try to frame him for murder?

Before he talked to Morris, he needed to speak to Litman again, see if the two had any connection. Reed walked over to the chief's office and rapped on the door. "Where's Litman now? Is he still in holding?"

"Yeah, why?"

"Because I need to ask him a few more questions."

"Is he still looking good for Silva's murder?"

Reed shook his head. "I don't think so, but I'll tell you more once I talk to him."

"All right. Let me know how it goes."

"I will.

Reed turned and headed down the long corridor toward holding. Maybe Litman had a connection that he didn't even know about, or maybe he did know and had refused to say anything. Either way, Reed was going to find out before he went to speak with Randall. He needed to be armed with answers when the man tried to twist everything to his advantage. Up until Taylor, Randall had made no mistakes. He was smart. Reed couldn't make any errors and allow the guy to walk. Too many people were counting on him to catch this killer.

With a ton of questions whirling around in his head, Reed walked into holding and saw Litman sitting on the bench next to another bald guy who was tatted up, some of his ink indicating skinhead involvement. His suspect looked totally uncomfortable in the man's presence. *Good.* This was Litman's first foray into prison life, and Reed would use that to get him talking.

An officer opened the door and called Litman's name. "Detective Brentwood would like a word with you."

Litman looked at Reed and released a breath. Clearly, something had transpired with his cell mate, and he was relieved to be getting away from him. Reed would let him go if he gave him some answers.

He led the man to an interrogation room. "Take a seat, Litman. You give me the answers I need, and I might let you go home. How does that sound?"

The look of pure relief had Reed stifling a smile.

Jerri Drennen

Litman wanted out of there, and Reed would use that to his advantage.

He sat across the table from the man, then slowly opened his notepad. "I only have a few questions. Ones I hope you can be honest about. "First, did you know Vince Silva personally?"

Litman started to swallow convulsively, clearly uncomfortable with the question. Why?

"Well?" Reed prompted, his eyes intent on Litman's.

"Yeah, I knew him. He was my personal trainer."

There was more to it. Reed could tell by the sweat forming on the man's upper lip. "How long had that relationship been going on?"

The man shrugged, trying to appear nonchalant. "Seven, eight months."

"And that's all it was? Client/personal training?"

The man started to fidget in his chair, accidently kicking the table leg. "Okay. So, it might have been more."

"More how?"

Litman's gave him a sneer. "We fucked, okay. Vince didn't want anyone to know because he was this guy's guy. He had an image to uphold. Women came to him, paid him big bucks to train them. They all swooned over him, hoping for what we had. He didn't want the truth to come out that he was gay."

"Did anyone else know about this relationship?"

"Maybe. Some guy walked in on us having a moment. I didn't know him. Seen him at the gym a few times right before that woman was attacked."

"Would you recognize him if you saw him again?"

"I don't know. Maybe."

He pulled out a photo of Morris.

"Could this be the guy?"

Litman studied the photo, then nodded. "Yeah, that's him. Are you saying this is the guy who killed Vince? Why would he do that? What did Vince do to him?"

"I'm not sure. I believe Vince might have discovered something this man didn't want him to know. He knew about your relationship with Vince, and I think he used that to distract the police from him."

"Are you going to get him? Make him pay for Vince's death?"

"I am. Thank you for coming clean. I know it couldn't have been easy. I'm going to have them release you now. I'm sorry for your loss."

Reed left, stopping off at the chief's to get him up to speed and start the paperwork for releasing Litman. Now, it was time to go meet a murderer and find a way to make him confess.

Chapter Twenty-Seven

Early evening, Taylor dozed on the couch, images of Reed floating around in her brain. *He was following someone down a staircase, the man in front of him wearing a dark suit. His hair was a dishwater blond, slicked back on his head with a greasy-looking substance.*

When they reached the bottom step, they made a left turn into a room that held a stainless-steel table, and beyond that was a huge walk-in door, also stainless steel. Were they in the morgue? It sort of looked like one.

The man turned and Taylor saw his face. His eyes were dark, almost menacing, his cheekbones sunk in like he'd lost a lot of weight. He was saying something to Reed, but she couldn't hear him. Then Reed spoke back, and the man's eyes narrowed, his mouth sneering. What had Reed said to upset him? Reed said something else. The man glanced down at his hand. Why? Wait. There was a ring on one of his fingers. Could Taylor somehow focus on that?

Suddenly the view zoomed in closer to his hand and she gasped. It was the killer's ring. Reed was with him.

She continued to watch their exchange, the man getting more agitated by the second. This made Taylor flinch. She knew what this guy could do.

That's when the man started inching his way back against a table, one of his hands reaching to grasp something. Taylor couldn't see. She wished she knew what Reed was doing. He'd left her view. Where was he?

The man said something, clearly shouting at Reed from what Taylor could tell. This exchange was going sideways fast.

Taylor wanted to turn away, but she was forced to watch. On alert. Waiting to see what happened next.

The man moved toward Reed, one of his hands held behind his back. Something bad was going to happen and she couldn't stop it.

Taylor woke with a start, her lungs burning in her chest. For some reason, she'd been holding her breath in her sleep.

She sat up, grabbed her phone, and scrolled to find Reed's number and pressed call. It rang six times before it went to voicemail. *Dammit.* Why wasn't he answering his phone? Was he all right? Had her attacker killed him? The mere thought made her want to vomit. She had to do something. Maybe this was one of those visions that she had before the event occurred. That was her hope. But where was Reed in the dream? And was it happening now, or would it occur sometime later?

Taylor had to figure all of this out. How had Reed talked her through seeing things she hadn't noticed before?

Step by step like he'd done.

First, what did she see when he'd started down the stairs. Were there any pictures, or papers that she noticed on the walls as he descended?

She watched the scene unfold, then observed a picture of that man with a plaque in his hand. It was an award of some kind. *Zoom in, Taylor. What does it say? Mortuary Director of the Year. Wow.* She had no idea they gave out awards for that. Name on the plaque. Morris Mortuary. That was where Reed was. At this funeral home. Now to find its location.

Taylor raced to get her laptop and found it was on Bremer Road. She had to get to Reed before it was too late. But first she had to get past the officer standing watch, or maybe he could help her save Reed. But would the officer believe her? Probably not. Best to not waste time trying to convince him. She had to go, and she had to go now.

She quickly dressed, threw on a pair of sneakers, and a jacket, then snuck to the back door. She'd need to get out fast because once she opened that door, an alarm would go off. Then she'd have to run as quickly as she could to find a cab to take her to the address. This was crazy. She knew that, but damned if she let Reed die if she could help prevent it.

She took a labored breath, then slipped the chain off, unbolted the lock and opened the door, sprinting through the backyard, thinking it best to stay off any path. That would be the first place the officer would look. She kept to the shadows for a couple of blocks, thankful that she was in good shape, otherwise this speed would have been impossible to sustain. When she thought it was safe, she ran to the street corner and calling for a rideshare. Luckily, it only took them ten minutes to arrive. Inside the car, she inhaled a ragged breath once they were on their way to the mortuary.

How was she going to get into the funeral home? What if it was locked? What would she do then? This whole thing was crazy. She didn't have a weapon to protect herself, let alone save Reed. Why hadn't she thought this thing through?

The cab came to a stop in front of a huge building, the sign on the place indicating it was the same as her dream. She paid the man and got out, and glanced around, spotting Reed's car in the parking area. Was she too late?

She raced to the front door, yanking only to find it locked. *Damn it*. Was there a back door? With a purpose, she sprinted around the building, finding the exit. What if it was also locked? There would be no way to help Reed.

She reached for the door, her heart rate hitching when it came open. Now, there was no turning back. Taylor was going inside, and she prayed she wasn't too late.

Once in the building, she needed to find those stairs to the basement floor. That was where they were.

As quietly as she could, she moved down a long hall to the front of the mortuary, keeping close to the wall. She came to the end of the hallway, a vestibule beyond, the left leading into one of the viewing rooms, a casket inside. *Ugh.* There were dead people here. Thank God they didn't die here, otherwise she'd probably start seeing them.

She shook off a sudden chill and took a right, inching her way down another short hallway, her skin erupting into goose bumps. This was the last place she wanted to be, but she had to save Reed. He had worked his way into her heart, and she couldn't lose him, even if he didn't have strong enough feelings to risk his job for her.

She turned and there it was, a small light above revealing the staircase going down. There was the picture. She stepped onto the first stair, her nerve endings tingling in her extremities. Reed would be the first person to tell her how stupid this was, yet she was going to do it anyway,

Halfway down, Taylor heard voices, one calm, the other angry. Reed and her attacker. She was getting closer to the man who had changed her life—who would have killed her if he'd had more time.

On the landing, she looked left, a light glowing from a door, slightly ajar. They were inside. The other man's voice got louder. This was in her dream. It was right before he started moving back to get that weapon. She had to stop him, had to change his trajectory, make Reed react sooner.

She raced to the door, pushing it open and screaming at the top of her lungs, "He's going for something on that tray. He's going to kill you, Reed."

Surprised, the man across the room hesitated just long enough for Reed to react.

The attacker charged forward, a long, sharp tool in his hand. He thrust it forward, narrowly missing Reed in the shoulder. He moved again, jabbing at Reed, his eyes full of rage, almost poking him in the side. He lunged again, but Reed shoved him back, his body bouncing off the table in the middle of the room.

While he was dazed, Reed reached for his sidearm and then pointed it at the man, "Don't even try it, Morris. Believe me, it'd be a pleasure to shoot you dead."

Instead of listening, he came at him again, forcing Reed to shoot him in the hand, causing him to scream and clutch at his wounded, bleeding fingers.

Reed kicked the weapon away and aimed his gun again at the man's head.

"Call 911. Tell them we need backup here, Taylor."

She did as instructed, adrenaline charging every cell in her body.

"How did you know to come here?" Morris asked.

"I've been dreaming about you since you attacked me."

His eyes widened. "I don't understand?"

"That makes two of us, then," she snapped back. "Why did you pick me? What did I ever do to you?"

He didn't answer, but she really didn't expect him to. That would be confessing, and he was clearly too smart to do that. Taylor just prayed they'd be able to find proof of what he'd done and put his evil ass away forever.

****

"Go ahead and take a seat, Taylor. I need to go talk with Morris." Reed smiled, then left her sitting at his desk.

So much was riding on getting the man to confess. A team was at the mortuary, looking for evidence. Reed didn't know if they'd find anything or not, which meant his job was paramount. He had to handle things just right.

He took a cleansing breath and stepped into the room. Randall looked like he was having a great time. What a psychopath. Reed hoped he'd at least be a little nervous. He still couldn't believe how Taylor had shown up. She was amazing and he thanked his lucky stars she had been given the gift she had. Otherwise, he might be dead.

He sat across from Morris and took out his notebook and pen. "So, Randall, care to talk about where you were on October tenth of last year."

"How the hell should I know? That was over six months ago."

"How about two weeks ago on the fifth. Remember what you were doing then? How about four days later on the ninth, or a few days after that on the twelfth?"

He simply shrugged, looking as if he hadn't a care in the world.

Reed was going to need to take another tactic. This was clearly not working.

"I did a little background check on you, Mr. Morris. I saw that you recently lost your mother. Care to tell me what happened there?"

Something in Randall's eyes changed. Reed had hit on an issue. *Okay.* So maybe the death of his mother had triggered his killing spree. But why?

"Did she die of natural causes?"

"That's fucking none of your business."

"Sorry. Did I hit a nerve, Randall? What type of relationship did you have with your mother?"

The man's demeanor changed, no longer calm as he started to fidget. Why would talking about his mother be so upsetting? Reed was going to have to delve a little deeper into the man's psyche, find out what it was about his mother that made him so nervous.

"Well," Reed prompted. "Did you love your mother, Randall?"

Something about that question made the man uncomfortable. What was going on in this guy's head?

Reed needed to keep digging. "Was your mother cruel to you, Randall? Overly critical, perhaps?"

He sneered at Reed. "Was yours?"

"I'm asking the questions here. I read that you lost your father when you were very young. It was just you and your mother in your formative years. I'm just trying to understand that relationship, Randall, and why you started killing women after your mother passed away.

Randall laughed and clenched his fists tight on top of the table. He thought killing Sylvia, Jamie, Ab and Vince was funny. *Fucking asshole.*

A knock sounded on the door, and Reed got up and left the room. Another detective stood outside, a folder in his hand. "What's this?" Reed asked.

"You are not going to believe it when you see it."

He handed the folder to him. "Be prepared, Reed. It's bad."

Reed opened the folder, the pictures inside making his stomach churn and his skin crawl. Then he sucked in a relieved breath.

Chapter Twenty-Eight

Taylor lugged her bag into her condo, Camila following directly behind her. Reed had returned to his desk an hour before to tell her that an officer was going to take her back to the safe house to pack her things so she could go home. Just hearing that made her happy, and now that she was here, she smiled brightly at her surroundings.

She helped her best friend settle into the guest bedroom and walked back to the kitchen to fix breakfast. Coffee was the first thing she needed, then maybe she'd work up the energy to make pancakes.

It was good to be in her own home, yet something plagued her. Would she ever see Reed again? Maybe at Randall Morris's trial, but how about before that happened? Nothing had been said between them. Did that mean something? Was not suggesting they get together an indicator of the end of the road with them?

She poured water into the top of the coffeemaker, filled the filter with coffee and switched it on. Taylor simply had to get back to her life and help Camila do the same. Her best friend was dealing with constant phone harassment from her husband, him refusing to let go, but at least Taylor and Camila had each other right now. That's all that mattered.

While she waited for the coffee to brew, her phone rang. It was Dean Ambrose and she answered.

"Taylor. Hello. I was hoping you'd be willing to go to that bar downtown to see if you can connect with the spirit you saw."

She was about to tell him no, but maybe this might just be what she needed to keep her mind off Reed.

"Okay. Sure. When were you thinking?"

"We could meet here and have lunch, then go and see what we could do to help this man cross over. So, around eleven thirty. Does that sound okay to you?"

"Sure. Is it okay if I bring a friend?"

He hesitated, then asked, "That detective?"

"No. My best friend Camila. She's staying with me right now, and I really don't want to leave her here alone. She's dealing with a lot."

"Of course. Bring her along. I'll see you soon, then."

Taylor ended the call, reached for two mugs, and filled them with coffee. Now, she needed to go and talk to Camila, warn her about what they were going to do and see if she'd be okay with it. Taylor didn't want to force her friend into a situation she might not be comfortable with. Reed hadn't dealt with it very well. Camila might have the same reaction.

She stepped into the spare room, finding her best friend crying. "What happened?"

"He keeps trying to call me." Camila wiped at her tears. "Then he texts me how much he loves me. He won't stop."

Taylor walked over and handed her friend a cup. "You could block him for a while, you know. At least until you figure out what you're going to do."

Camila took a sip of coffee. "I already know what I'm going to do. I'm going to get a divorce as soon as possible and get on with my life. Gavin can deal with the fallout from both of our families since he was the one who couldn't keep it in his pants and now has the evidence growing inside another woman."

She had to give her best friend props. When Camila made up her mind, it was set in stone. Taylor was more back and forth, something she'd need to work on.

"So, I got a call from that man who is dealing with the same thing I am. I think I told you about him."

"Dean something or other, right? Camila asked.

"He wants to get together and drive downtown to that bar I saw in my dream and later went to. Where I saw that one guy dressed in old-fashioned clothing. We want to find out why he's there and try to help him cross over. Would you be up for tagging along?"

Her friend's eyes lit up. "Yes, I would love to. You forget how much I love the paranormal."

"Great. So, it's a date. Finish your coffee and then join me in the kitchen. I'm going to make your favorite, pancakes."

"What would I do without you?"

"I feel the same. Thank God we have one another."

Taylor returned to the kitchen and got all the ingredients she'd need to mix up some batter. She had to keep herself busy otherwise Reed would slip into her thoughts again. At least, he'd made sure her car had been sitting in her driveway and that she and Camila wouldn't have to take a rideshare to Dean's. He was always on top of things—so efficient, and reliable, and sexy, and….

Taylor was in love with him. Dammit. She was in love with a man who didn't feel enough for her to risk everything. How was she going to deal with that?

****

Reed stepped into the morgue, his stomach sickened

by what the forensic team found at the funeral home. Randall Morris was a very disturbed individual, though it seemed to have been fed by the man's mother.

"Hey, Ken, what did you find out?"

"I'm still waiting on DNA on those parts, but they were sewn onto the dead women's body. I think from what I could check, it looks like Cynthia Morris, Randall's mother, who died of cancer close to a year ago. She'd been in the deep freeze that long."

"In other words, there is no body in the coffin that was buried."

"Like I said, we have to wait for DNA, but that's my assumption."

"Why would he do something like this? It doesn't make any sense."

"Maybe a psych evaluation is warranted here. Since something triggered this inside the man."

"At the very least." Reed shook his head.

"I'll let you know when I get the results back."

"All right. Thanks." Reed stepped out of the room, on his way to see the suspect again. He was going to have to ask some uncomfortable questions, and he wasn't sure how to begin.

He'd dealt with strange things before, but usually they weren't this bizarre.

Outside the interrogation room, he took a calming breath, then opened the door and stepped inside. Randall sat motionless in the chair, appearing as if he was simply there to talk.

Reed took a seat across from him. "Can I get you anything? Coffee? Maybe some water?"

He shook his head. "I'll be out of here soon."

Randall was caught dead to rights, and he thought

he'd be a free man. Talk about delusional.

"I have a few more questions for you first, Randall."

He eyed Reed like he was a fly he wanted to swat. "Ask them so I can get out of here."

"So, what kind of relationship did you have with your mother?"

Randall started to laugh. "What are you, a shrink now?"

"Do you think you may need one?" Reed watched the man intently.

He shrugged. "Doesn't everyone? I mean, in this day and age, seems that every person has a little crazy in them. Even you, Detective."

"But I didn't kill anyone."

Randall sat back in his chair and crossed his arms over his chest, flinching when he bumped his bandaged hand. His face grimaced.

Reed was going to have to get to the point with him. "Did you have a normal childhood, Randall?"

He sneered at him. "What's normal?"

Reed smiled at the man. Randall knew what he was trying to imply but didn't seem to care.

"What was life like with your mother?"

"Life like? What do you mean? My mother loved me, like every other mother loves their children?"

"Were you upset when she died?"

"Were you upset when yours did? Of course, I was upset. Most people are when they lose a loved one. I see it every day in my line of work."

"True, but most don't keep their bodies after they've passed and sew other women's body parts onto them, Randall. Why did you do that?"

He turned away, not answering.

"Okay, here is what I think happened, Randall. I think for whatever reason, you just couldn't let go of your mother. I don't know why, and frankly, I don't want to know. You kept her body frozen and wanted her to look like she did before she was sick, so you found women who looked like her. You killed them, cut off the parts that your mother had lost and transferred them to her body. What do you think? Am I getting anything wrong in my assessment?"

The look he gave Reed would have iced over the whole southern hemisphere. The man needed help, and hopefully he'd get some in prison. If he didn't get the death penalty.

"Well?" Reed prompted. "I'm waiting on what I got wrong, Randall."

"Fuck you, Detective."

"You know, I sort of feel sorry for you. Your mother clearly dominated your life, and in doing so, created a monster. Maybe we'd be willing to ask for leniency if you cooperate. That's completely up to you, Randall. Now, what do you say? Want to make a deal or not?"

He sat back and smiled. "Or not."

Reed would love to haul off and punch the smug look off his face but refrained. The man probably thought the death penalty wouldn't apply to this case or maybe he *wanted* to die to be with that thing he called mother. She was hardly that, yet this man idolized her.

"Last question, Randall. What's with the ring?"

"It was a gift."

"From your mother?" Reed asked.

Randall spun the band on his finger, then looked at Reed and smiled again. "I want to call my lawyer. I'm done talking."

"Suit yourself. I'll see you in court. Oh, by the way, most inmates in prison hate women killers. Good luck in there while you await trial."

The smile left the man's face, and Reed turned, smirking as he exited the room.

Chapter Twenty-Nine

Taylor and Camila stepped onto the porch of Dean Ambrose's house and rang the doorbell. When he answered, the hairs on Taylor's arms charged. What was causing it?

Camila frowned. "Everything okay?"

"I just got a strange feeling right before you got here. Not sure why. I think we should skip lunch and head downtown if that's all right with you?"

"That's fine. Camila and I had a big breakfast anyway. Are we taking your car or mine?"

"We'll take mine since I've already programmed the address into my navigational system, and we are ready to go."

Taylor sat in the front passenger seat, unsure if she'd even question that strange feeling Dean had spoken about. But bad feelings usually meant something to her. Surely, to him as well. Should she ask him what he thought it could be or let it lie for now? Maybe they could talk about it on the way back. Right now, she needed to think about the man they were going to see. What type of questions did she need to ask him, and then how did she find a way to get him to cross over like they'd done for Ab?

"So, Dean," Camila said from the back seat. "How long have you had your gift?"

"Almost seven years now. I was in a bad car

accident. When I came to, I remembered all these people standing around me, telling me I needed to go back. That I had work to do. The first time I experience something supernatural, I was out having lunch with a friend and this person who was sitting next to me kept trying to get my attention, a young man my friend couldn't see. That fact scared me. The more it happened, the more the spirits could connect with me. That first young man just stared. Didn't say a word. Now, they talk to me. Tell me their stories, and I help them try to figure out why they're still on this plane."

"Do you ever regret being given this gift?" Taylor knew this was her life going forward.

He frowned. "I'm sometimes bothered that they pop in when I'm trying to have an actual life. Dating is hard when the woman you're seeing doesn't understand your abilities, resents them. I had a fiancée when my accident happened. She couldn't deal with me seeing dead people. It weirded her out. She said it was unnatural and that she couldn't marry me because of it. I was angry about the gift then. I got over it. I guess I had no choice, and neither do you, Taylor. You can try to block it out, but then bad shit happens."

Taylor's eyes widened. "What kind of bad stuff?"

Turn left at the next exit, his navigational system said, causing her to jump and then to focus on the bar that would be just around the next turn.

Taylor pointed to it ahead and he pulled into a spot and cut the engine. "Let's just go in and have a drink, see if the man shows himself. If he does, let him lead. See if he starts talking. If he does, then you can ask questions. We need to know why he's pulled to this place and what's keeping him here."

They all exited and entered the bar, the same putrid smell churning Taylor's stomach.

"Which booth did you see him in?" Dean asked from beside her.

She pointed to one that was empty. "Let's go sit there and see what happens."

Camila and Taylor sat on the opposite side of Dean and where she'd seen the man sitting. If he was there, she wanted to face him.

A different waitress stepped over to them. "What can I get you?"

"I'll have a light beer," Dean said.

"I'll have one too." Camila smiled at the waitress.

"Make it three," Taylor reiterated.

When she'd gone, Dean asked, "Do you feel anything?"

"Not yet, but when we first arrived that day, I didn't see him at this booth. We sat at the bar, then I turned around and he was there. He stared at me, and I turned back around. I then got a cold chill, and looked again, and he was gone."

Dean smiled. "Sounds like he passed through you. That's good. He has a connection to you now. That should help us."

The waitress brought their beers and left.

Taylor poured hers into a glass and then took a long swallow. She needed something to calm her, and she hoped the alcohol would help.

What if the man didn't show up? What if she'd imagined the whole thing? As she was taking another drink, a cold draft hit her and caused goose bumps to erupt all over her body. She glanced around the room, thinking he was there somewhere, then a mist formed next to Dean and the man appeared, his eyes narrowing on her.

Taylor gulped, thinking he didn't look happy to see her.

Dean's face scared her further. He turned his head and his mouth gaped slightly. He clearly saw him too.

"What's going on? Camila asked them.

"He's here." Taylor gulped. "And let's just say, he doesn't look happy to see me."

Taylor wished she was anywhere but here at that moment. The first time she'd seen this man, he hadn't given off these bad feelings, but now, he was eyeing her like he wanted her dead.

"This is bad," Dean said barely above a whisper. "This is not a good spirit. He's angry and I've never dealt with an angry ghost before. Perhaps we should get up and leave."

A wailing sound pierced Taylor's eardrums and both her and Dean covered their ears. "He doesn't want us to leave," Dean said to Camila, who looked confused.

"Do you think he'll harm us if we try?" Taylor asked, then the torturous sound finally stopped. "I mean, can he even do that?"

Dean shrugged. "This is above my experience. I'm not sure."

Taylor swallowed hard. "Okay, so maybe we need to find out why he's so angry."

Right when she was about to ask, her cell phone chirped. She glanced at it, seeing that it was Reed asking where she was. That he'd come by to see her, and she wasn't there.

She quickly texted him back. —*went to see the ghost at the bar. Things are tense. Ghost is mad.*—

—On my way— popped up on her screen.

Taylor took in a relieved breath. Reed was coming—her knight in shining armor—the man who always made her feel safe. What more could she ask for.

****

Reed took in a calming breath, not sure what he'd find when he stepped inside the bar. All he knew was, Taylor was in danger, and he needed to get to her.

He pulled the door open and stepped inside, smoke and alcohol permeating the air. Wasn't there a law against smoking in a public place? Clearly, they weren't abiding by that. When his vision adjusted to the lighting, he glanced around and saw Taylor sitting at a booth with Dean Ambrose and Camila. Why was he here? Trying to score points? *Asshole.*

Reed would take care of him later. Right now, Taylor looked terrified by something.

He walked over, happy to see her eyes light up when she saw him. There was something between them, but was it strong enough for them to just be friends until Randall Morris was convicted? There couldn't be a sexual relationship until then or he'd lose his job. This was why he'd come by to see her. To talk to her about it. To find out if she was willing to wait for them to be together.

Now, Dean Ambrose could very well throw a wrench into the whole thing.

"What's going on?" he asked, looking at her.

Taylor pointed to the empty seat. "The man is here, and he's not happy with me for some reason."

Reed looked over at the spot next to Dean. "Have you tried asking him why?"

"Yeah. All he would say is I stayed away too long."

Reed frowned. "It's only been a few days. Have you asked his name? Maybe that could help us figure out what's going on."

Dean snorted, drawing his attention to him.

"What?"

"Of course, we asked. This is not my first rodeo, Detective."

Reed stared at Dean, pissed that he was trying to impress Taylor with his bravado. If he was such a brave guy, then why had Taylor asked him to come save them? "What did he tell you it was?"

"Michael Kerns," Dean said in a sharp tone. "He was born in nineteen twenty-three and died in nineteen forty-nine. Murdered. That's why he's so angry."

"Who killed him and why?"

"That he couldn't tell me. What he did say it was all because of a woman, who he thinks is Taylor, or that waitress that looks like her."

"Angie," Taylor said. "That's why he was so angry with me. Angie hasn't been here since her attack."

"So, this ghost can't tell you two apart? You look similar but not alike."

"Spirits don't differentiate like we do. Faces are hazy to them."

"Okay. So, what does he want from Taylor, then?" Reed asked.

"He wants her to find his killer. He knows that it had something to do with this woman all those years ago. Can you see if you can't find anything on this guy's death? Learn if they had any leads in his murder at the time?"

"I guess I can try, but I can't promise anything. That would be a very cold case."

Taylor smiled at him and caused a certain part of his body to react. He wanted her with every fiber of his being. But how did she feel? He didn't know, but he sure as hell wasn't going to sit back and wait for Dean Ambrose to step in and claim her. Not when the two had so much in common.

Maybe trying to solve this case would keep them together, both working to find clues to solve the mystery, and discover who the woman was and whether she had been the catalyst to murder. It was a way to see Taylor on a regular basis until Randall Morris was convicted and sentenced to prison. Then he could be with her the way he so badly wanted to be. Reed just had to make sure Dean didn't get in the way before that day came.

"We should work together on this," Reed said, then gave her a smile.

She nodded. "I'd like that more than anything and I'd love to start tomorrow if you're free."

He leaned down and whispered in her ear, "I'll make sure I am."

A word about the author...

Jerri Drennen is an author of romantic suspense as well as paranormal and contemporary romance. Growing up on a farm in a tiny town in Minnesota was where she started reading romance and learned how to make up stories in her head. After meeting her husband, she moved to his hometown in Missouri where she now live with one of their four children. Her kids call her the crazy cat lady.

www.ingramcontent.com/pod-product-compliance
Lightning Source LLC
Chambersburg PA
CBHW070109030726
47506CB00002B/665